TARGETED VIOLENCE

A NICK LAWRENCE NOVEL

BRIAN SHEA

Severn River
PUBLISHING

Severn River Publishing
www.SevernRiverPublishing.com

This is a work of fiction. Names, characters, businesses, places, events and incidents are either the products of the author's imagination or used in a fictitious manner. Any resemblance to actual persons, living or dead, or actual events is purely coincidental.

ISBN: 978-1-951249-25-0 (Paperback)

ALSO BY BRIAN SHEA

The Nick Lawrence Series

Kill List

Pursuit of Justice

Burning Truth

Targeted Violence

Murder 8

The Boston Crime Thriller Series

Murder Board

Bleeding Blue

The Penitent One

Never miss a new release! Sign up to receive exclusive updates from author Brian Shea.

BrianChristopherShea.com/Newsletter

Sign up and receive a free copy of

Unkillable: A Nick Lawrence Short Story

This book is dedicated to Barbara. You are my silent partner in this endeavor and have supported and nurtured my work. I'm forever grateful for all you do, and I'm blessed to call you my friend.

1

Sheldon Price stood outside the main doors of Connerton-Jacobs High School as he'd done at the beginning of each day for the last three years. He knew this would be the last time he would ever set foot inside its halls. The gangly, rail-thin junior stopped a few feet from the main door. The mottled reflection in the tinted glass doors stared back at him. His matted hair, glasses, and pimple-riddled face had only given more ammo to the arsenal of verbal abuse he'd endured every day since beginning his arduous journey into adolescence. The kindest of his abusive peers had called him Smelly Shelly, but there were many other names, each salt on the open wound of his psyche. He tried not to yield to its pain and found the old adage about sticks and stones was a load of crap. Words hurt. More times than he cared to admit he had curled into a ball on the floor of his bedroom and cried until his tear ducts emptied.

His father had left when Sheldon turned twelve. Not that his presence in his life would've added any balance. Being an All-American football player, his father never understood Sheldon's plight. His father was disappointed, more like disgusted, by his son's physical weakness. At times, early in his life, his father had openly mocked Sheldon's poor performance in all things sports related. *I guess the "awesome" gene skipped a generation*, his father had told a neighbor. Sheldon had overheard the comment and its impact still resonated to this day.

Sheldon's mother was a different story altogether. Sheldon had become the man of the house after his father's departure, and he cared for her on those days when she couldn't get off the couch. She'd slipped into a deep depression and never recovered. Her condition worsened when she began using sleeping pills to stay in a semi-comatose state. Sheldon did the grocery shopping, cooked the meals, cleaned the house, and even took a job as a stock boy at Jenkin's Hardware to float the bills when his father decided not to send his monthly stipend, which was becoming more frequent.

He looked at his reflection. *Man of the house*, he thought. He wondered who would look after her and worried that what he was about to do on this beautiful early spring day in Jessup, Tennessee, might be the final nail in her rapidly closing coffin. He shuddered, trying to shake the thought from his head. She would be devastated, but he'd left her a letter that would hopefully provide her some comfort in the coming aftermath.

His momentary lapse into introspection was interrupted by an unexpected impact. Sheldon's body lurched forward, almost causing him to topple. Staggering, he caught himself before face planting into the concrete.

Then he heard the all-too-familiar accompaniment from an all-too-familiar voice, "What's that smell?"

The shove had caused the last reserve of hesitation to dissipate from Sheldon's mind. His commitment resolved. He turned to face his attacker.

His eyes flashed with anger at the sight of Blake Tanner.

Blake hadn't always been this way. Sadly, Sheldon and Blake spent many an afternoon playing and exploring in the expanse of their neighborhood creek-fed woods. That was years ago and the memory of those days had faded into oblivion. The thick-shoul-dered athletic boy standing before him held no resemblance to his childhood friend.

"Oh look at this! Smelly Shelly looks angry. Hey, Dom, do you think he wants to fight?" Blake said.

"I really hope so," Dominic Purcell said. "Tell you what. We'll even let you take the first swing."

Sheldon stood still, but underneath the loose-fitting T-shirt his body trembled with fear. Like sharks after blood in the water, Blake and Dom circled him, closing the distance. Their breath smelled of toaster strudel and orange juice. The sweet smell contradicted the savage look in their eyes. Sheldon moved slightly, clutching his backpack's strap draped over his left arm.

"He's trembling. Look at him. He's probably going to piss himself," Blake said through gritted teeth.

"Great idea. How about you piss your pants right now and I won't cave your face in," Dom said balling his fist.

Sheldon felt his face warm in anger.

"You heard him. Do it!" Blake said, leaning in. A wide smile stretched across his flawless face.

Blake suddenly stepped back and his whole appearance changed as the school's secretary, Ms. Turtley approached. "Good morning, Miss Turtley."

"Good morning, boys," she said, glancing at the trio. Her eyes rested a second longer on Sheldon.

Sheldon was on the verge of tears. A blind person could see that the exchange taking place was not an amicable one, but she barely broke stride and continued into the school. He'd seen it too many times to count. The faculty seemed to look the other way when it came to Sheldon's abuse. Just like his father, most had probably never experienced his pain and had no reference for it. Or worse, they had been the Blakes and Doms in their own high school years and saw it as some twisted rite of passage.

"So, how about it? Is Dom going to pop those zits on your face with his fist or are you going to piss those pants?" Blake asked.

Sheldon weighed his options. His backpack now seemed heavier, and his mind raced for a solution. He knew that Dom would follow through with his threat. It wouldn't be the first time. Facing the unbeatable odds, he yielded and released his bladder. The warmth spread out from his underwear, permeating the front of his jeans. It quickly cooled in the early morning spring air.

"Holy crap! He pissed his pants!" Dom yelled.

Other students cast looks as they passed by into the school.

"Smelly Shelly pissed his pants!" Blake yelled, calling further attention.

Sheldon listened to the laughter as classmates passed by, pointing and gawking. The only thing he could do was fight back against the well of emotion and prevent the tears so desperately pleading for their release.

Blake and Dom gave each other a high five and chest bump while running into the school, but not before snapping a picture on their phones. Another viral Sheldon picture that would reach every kid before Sheldon made it to his first class. He exhaled, collecting himself. Today would be different. Soon they would understand.

Sheldon allowed his current circumstance to solidify his resolve. The need to cry had subsided. On any other day he would have turned and made the long, embarrassing walk home. He had tallied an impressive number of absences over the last three years, but nobody seemed concerned.

The second bell rang, the tardy bell, and Sheldon remained outside the school, staring at his reflection in the doors, the front of his khaki pants now darkened with urine. He looked at himself and wondered if he would survive. Part of him hoped that he didn't.

2

I'm not Smelly Shelly, not anymore. I'm Sasquatch_187. I'm the warrior elite and today I will cross over and become a legend. The first selected and hand-picked from a sea of others to make the leap, Sheldon thought to himself. A tenuous smile crept across his acne-covered face.

Sheldon's hand trembled as he gripped the metal handle of the front door to Connerton-Jacobs High School. He knew that once the door opened, everything would change forever. There would be no going back.

He'd been told fear was to be expected, but the reward would be unimaginable. He was a Patriot. He was the first soldier in a new war.

One deep breath and he jerked the handle as he exhaled loudly, almost grunting. The door resisted slightly, the suction from the weather-stripping released, and Sheldon stepped inside, entering into the main hallway. The overhead lights bounced off the heavily waxed laminate tile flooring, casting a soft glow. Purple and gold, the colors of the Connerton-Jacobs Cougars, covered the lockers lining the hallway. Those colors would forever cause his stomach to turn, and the sight of them now added fuel to his hatred of the place.

An obnoxiously loud squeak accompanied each step of Sheldon's left foot, his puddle of urine had soaked his left sneaker. His worn sneakers barely had any tread left, and coupled with the wetness, he moved more gingerly, taking shorter steps to accommodate for this. His backpack remained slung over his shoulder and, in the quiet of the empty hall, its contents banged loudly. He laughed, envisioning himself as a one-man band. A silly thought, that on other days, would have provided some degree of mental escape from his current circumstance. Sheldon could not allow his mind to drift. The plan was simple enough, but its execution would require his absolute focus.

He stopped in his tracks. At the far end of the hall he saw Darryl Hawthorne, the school security guard. Sheldon froze, hoping the barrel-chested man wouldn't notice him.

To his dismay Officer Hawthorne turned, smiled and waved. Hawthorne had interrupted many of Sheldon's bullying incidents and was probably the only person in the school who seemed to be looking out for him. The deep voice of the middle-aged guard had sent students running, though Sheldon knew he was a gentle giant.

"Hey, Sheldon," Hawthorne said with a broad smile. The whiteness of his teeth contrasted with the darkness of his skin and black, stubbled beard. "A little late this morning—oh damn, what happened?" Hawthorne's eyes had obviously caught sight of the pants.

Sheldon swallowed hard and failed to answer the big man. His nervousness caused him to sway anxiously, even though he knew Hawthorne wasn't a threat.

"How about we get you to the nurse's office? Maybe call your mom and get you a change of clothes?" Hawthorne asked with genuine concern. He began closing the distance to Sheldon.

Sheldon regained his composure. "No thanks Officer Hawthorne. I've got a pair of sweatpants in my gym locker," Sheldon said quickly.

It was a lie. Sheldon never dared to go into the dreaded boys' locker room, and on gym days would resign to wearing his sweaty attire all day. Thus one of the reasons he'd earned the nickname Smelly Shelly. It was a price he was willing to endure because he knew, for a boy like Sheldon Price, entering the boys' locker room would be the equivalent of a zebra entering a lion's den just before feeding time.

"Alright, just make sure you stop by the office and grab a hall pass before heading on to your first period."

"Will do," Sheldon said. As Hawthorne began walking away Sheldon called out to him. "Officer Hawthorne, thanks for always being kind to me."

"Sure thing, buddy," Hawthorne said, turning and walking away in the opposite direction.

Sheldon hated everything about this school. The design layout had all of the eight corridors converging to one central common area, referred to as the Commons.

The Commons had an octagonal design. Three steps brought students down to a smattering of couches, benches, and tables for them to study and socialize for the ten minutes between classes. It was roughly one hundred feet across and, for the socially accepted, the Commons served as a hangout. Sheldon's schedule forced him into the Commons several times a day during the transitions. Popular kids loved it and reveled in the few minutes of socialization before the next block of instruction, but to kids in Sheldon's ranks it was a guaranteed block of public humiliation. Not today though. And never again.

Today the two hundred and twelve students of Connerton-Jacobs High School would learn a terrible lesson.

3

The Commons was vacant. Typically, few people lingered in the space during the first instructional block of the day. In the absence of other students Sheldon felt at ease. It was a strange sensation and one he'd not experienced previously.

Sheldon walked into the center and sat on a bright red couch, a spot reserved for only the most popular students. He knew the soft fabric would absorb some of the urine, and he rejoiced in the thought of some unsuspecting popular kid sitting in Smelly Shelly's piss. He unshouldered the backpack and rested it on the floor in front of him. It was heavy, but unlike normal days, it contained no books or notebooks.

He looked down at his watch. He had ten minutes until the bell would ring, releasing the horde of the student body into the hallways for class transition. He unzipped the backpack and peered inside. The instructions had been clear and simple. *Set it on the ground. Flip the switch to activate. Press the green button on the remote to detonate.*

Sheldon looked around and was pleased to see that the halls leading into the Commons remained vacant. He looked up at the black convex lens of the security camera and smiled for posterity.

He knew that Officer Hawthorne was the only person who monitored the cameras and knew, seeing him only minutes before, that he was out conducting his rounds. He slid the heavy metallic frame of the device from his pack and gently put it beside the couch, toggling the switch upward. It hummed and a red light came on.

Sheldon dug his hand into the bag and retrieved the remote. He then went back into the backpack and removed the last item, his mother's Smith and Wesson M&P 9mm semiautomatic handgun. She had bought it the month after his father left them. She told Sheldon it was for home defense, but the gun sat in a shoebox on the top shelf of her closet. He took it a month ago and she'd never noticed. It came with a spare magazine which he had filled to capacity. Sheldon had never actually fired a real gun, but Sasquatch_187 was a pro. *How hard could the real thing be?*

The empty backpack now loosely covered the device and he slipped into position, tucking himself into a far corner hidden by a locker. He hoped it would provide enough shielding from the blast.

The gun felt heavy in his hand. The extra magazine was stuffed in his damp front pocket.

He waited.

4

_____

The bell rang. The sound interrupted the silence and startled him, causing his pulse to quicken. Then he heard the sound he was waiting for. A loud rumbling filled the hallways. The eight arteries feeding into the Commons reverberated with the bang of lockers and voices. He felt a wave of nausea wash over him at the thought of what he was preparing to do, but the laughter of several students nearby quickly reminded him of why he was doing this. The first few students entered. His instructions had been to wait as long as he could. The Commons filled. No one noticed Sheldon wedged in the corner. This fact didn't shock him. He often felt as though he were a ghost moving among the living.

Couches were quickly filled by students that didn't care about the ten-minute time constraint allocated for socialization before scurrying off to their next class.

Sabrina Wilmont, Blake's girlfriend of the month, sat in the exact spot Sheldon had just occupied moments before. He watched as her nose curled and she gave an exaggerated sniff of her surroundings as she looked for the source. Her face contorted in disgust as she shot up from the couch and screamed, patting her butt. Blake stood nearby and began laughing at her. His laughter activated Sheldon Price's internal time bomb and he stepped out from the corner, revealing himself.

Without saying a word, he raised the gun, pointing it in the direction of Blake Tanner. He heard a ripple of screams from students seeing the threat, but the beating of his heart seemed to drown out the noise. Sheldon squeezed the trigger. With each kick of the gun he aimed in a different direction.

"Sasquatch 187!" He screamed his war cry, bellowing wildly.

His classmates began running, ducking, and screaming as they tried to predict the next volley of shots. Sheldon continued clicking several times before he realized the gun was empty. He reached into his pocket, frantically grabbing for the spare magazine. In his haste he mistakenly put his hand into the pocket containing the detonator. Before his mind comprehended the error, his finger hand depressed the green button.

The Commons erupted in a bright light immediately followed by a deafening bang, cancelling his ability to see or hear. Sheldon was no longer standing. The blast had knocked him into the corner and his head struck the metal of the locker he'd hidden behind. The secondary impact with the locker had propelled him forward onto the floor. The laminate flooring no longer shined and his reflection was distorted by the blood pooling out from him.

Sasquatch_187 was gone and Smelly Shelly stared back, scared and dying, until his eyes closed to emptiness.

5

It was cold. Not a cold that any thermostat or workout could fix. It projected from within his heart and coated his bones. The room's endless gray added to it. The only color came from the faded orange binding of the one book he kept on his otherwise empty shelf. The timeless words of Sun Tzu had been committed to memory, the book now only served as a reminder of its teachings.

Nick stretched his body and gazed at the ceiling, retracing the cracks as he'd done a thousand times before. The maze of coils designed to support his frame penetrated the cot's thin mattress, poking at him like a blind acupuncturist with a penchant for pain. He'd already gone through his morning workout routine and figured he would get in another round of exercise before his next meal.

The last year had been the hardest of his life. And Nick Lawrence knew hard. The first few months of confinement had left him depleted, sleeping most of the day and barely eating. During his trial he'd lost nearly thirty pounds. Each time he closed his eyes he willed himself to die. Each time he woke he realized it wouldn't be that easy. He'd been shot, blown up, and stabbed, so starvation seemed an unlikely cause of death for someone with his uncanny ability to survive.

One morning he woke to the silence of his surroundings and understood that he had died. At least a death in the proverbial sense. His trial had ended. Nick, a former agent with the FBI, was convicted of five counts of murder. The woman who had brought the case against Nick was a far deadlier killer than he ever was, but she'd amassed a treasure trove of evidence against him.

Nick suffered greatly at the hands of that woman. She destroyed him, tearing away any connection to the people he loved. She'd managed to disguise herself as a man and slip into his mother's medical facility. His sweet loving mother, whose recall of life's joys had mostly been washed away by the spreading decay of her dementia, was killed by this madwoman. His mother was the last living member of his once close-knit family. Her murder had initially eluded investigators, but DNA had tied her to the crime.

More devastating than his mother's murder was the loss of Anaya and their unborn child. Anaya hadn't died, but after losing their child something inside him died, and she never forgave Nick for what happened. The strength of their love was tested and failed.

A lifetime of service to his country cut down by the judicial process. He'd killed Montrose and several of his henchmen. At the time, it made sense. Killing Montrose was justice served for the young girls' lives he'd destroyed. The same system that had failed to convict a human trafficker had no problem in closing the case on Nick.

The guilty verdict was delivered after Nick's plea, and he was handed his sentence, destined to serve out the remaining years of his life with the types of criminals he'd worked so hard to put away. On the judgment day, eight months ago, he was reborn. Everything he had was taken, ripped from his hands. What was left was an empty vessel, and he committed to never losing again.

Since his rebirth Nick had regained the lost thirty pounds and added close to fifteen more, all of which was muscle. It was amazing what you could do in a six by ten space when you put your mind to it.

Nick rolled off of his cot, landing in a push-up position. His long hair flopped forward as he warmed up his joints with a quick thirty, and then he began putting in the work that would occupy the next forty-five minutes of intensity. Each workout focused on different muscle groups, enabling him to attack every session.

He'd not cut his hair or shaved his beard since the day he entered Masterson Federal Correctional Facility. His attorney had warned him about his appearance, saying that the judge would see him as a savage. Nick knew his case was a lost cause. Simmons had collected an impressive amount of evidence against him. It also didn't help when he, against his lawyer's recommendation, pleaded guilty to the murder of five people. Five consecutive life sentences later, Nick was still alive.

Time had been a cruel gift. Each ticking second carried its own life sentence. Nick had no cellmate. None of the inmates in D Wing did. The justice system had deemed his neighbors to be unfit for the general population, or gen pop, due to the violent nature of their crimes or the volatility of their psychological makeup. Nick apparently fell into both categories but knew the deeper rationale in placing him in relative isolation was because he'd been FBI, a fact that wouldn't be lost on some of the residents. It would be a huge feather in the cap of any inmate capable of sticking a broken piece of plastic into his neck.

Only twice a day were the prisoners of D Wing allowed to mingle, during the lunch meal and the games hour. Some psychologist had the genius idea of putting a group of killers together to play chess. Obviously, this person had never spent an evening of deep conversation with Bill "the Blade" Culver, who spent his twenty-two hours of isolation three doors down from Nick.

Nick knew Culver's story, as did most of the world. Culver had carved his way through thirty-seven known victims. He was selective in most of his attacks but sometimes rage got the best of him and impulse took over. It was for that reason he'd been caught.

In a moment of road rage, Culver had killed a Georgia State Trooper. The incident was caught on the dash camera and its brutality made him a legend. He had been shot by the Trooper, but it didn't stop Culver. He managed to disarm the lawman and used the Trooper's gun to beat him to death. The most disturbing scene in the video occurred when Culver stood, blood covered, and smiled at the camera. That image had been plastered all over the Internet. During a rare and candid interview Culver was asked why he killed the trooper and his answer was eerily simple, "Because I could." Among the prison population he was notorious. His large, three-hundred-pound frame was given wide berth when on the move. Although a disproportionate amount of his girth was comprised of fat, he was strong and surprisingly quick. Nick had witnessed him on more than one occasion address a newcomer who, unknowingly, crossed his path.

A newbie, some tough-looking skinhead, had bumped Culver accidentally while moving past him during the lunch wave. Before the guards could react, Culver had snatched the man by the neck and slammed him to the ground. While the guards attempted to separate the large man from his toppled prey, Culver had managed to crush the Neo-Nazi prisoner's windpipe. It was a devastating attack and was over within seconds.

Culver managed to avoid the death penalty by making a trade. He'd given the locations of one of his previous victim's gravesites in exchange for life. A grieving family's need for closure trumped a judicial need to execute a killer. And so, Bill "the Blade" Culver had guaranteed he would be a lifelong member of Masterson's D Wing.

Nick sat on his cot allowing the sweat to drip freely from his face, forming a small pool in the space between his white sneakers. There was no clock in any of the D Wing cells and no clocks on any of the walls. Inmates were not permitted to have watches and therefore had no reference for the passing of time. The only discernible timeline came in the way of the light and bell system. The lights came on every morning, announcing the start to a new day, and turned off after the lights-out warning every night, signaling its end. Each meal was announced by loudspeaker after a buzzer sounded. It was a recorded message and therefore never deviated in tone or content. Breakfast's and dinner's message directed prisoners to turn from the door and place their hands on the wall. If you complied, the meal slot, located at the base of the heavy steel door, would lift and the beige tray would slide into the cell. Inmates were not permitted to move until the meal door was closed. Anyone that refused to put their hands on the walls or failed to hold their position didn't get fed.

In the early days of his confinement, Nick tested the waters by not complying with the recorded directive. He lost many meal opportunities in those first months, which was one of the reasons he'd lost so much weight. The guards did not treat him differently from the others in D Wing. He respected the principle of that, but also came to the realization he was by all accounts a prisoner. Nothing more, nothing less.

The lunch wave and recreation block had a different announcement. The buzzer sounded and the announcement to hold the wall was given, but unlike the click of the meal door during breakfast and dinner, inmates had to wait for the loud hiss and clank of the cell door to release. The doors would then slide open and inmates would be instructed to release their hold and step outside their cell. Guards would line the octagonal balcony at strategic points. The cells were housed on the second tier of D Wing, approximately ten feet above the space below, used for lunch and the board games hour of recreational time. The area used for lunch and games was adorned with heavy aluminum tables and chairs bolted to the poured concrete floor.

The buzzer sounded and was quickly followed by the announcement. *Inmates, step up and place your hands on the wall. Keep your eyes facing the wall until told to move.* Nick took up his position, placing his hands on the gray wall. He had done this so many times, he'd become convinced his hands had weathered a divot out of the rough concrete.

The next command given was fifteen seconds after the first. *Inmates, turn and face the open door. Keep your hands at your side and exit your cell.* Nick turned to face the open door and then upon direction, stepped to the landing outside his cell. Head straight and body rigid, in a prison version of the military position of attention, Nick waited until told to move. The robotic command was given, *Face inward and maintain your interval.* The remaining instructions would be provided by the guards evenly spaced along the tier, shepherding the convicts.

Nick wondered what today's mystery meat would be. Food no longer carried any semblance of taste. It was now only fuel for his body, for the machine.

He maintained his place in the line. Each inmate was to move through the chow line with no less than three feet in front and behind, shuffling slowly forward. This was to prevent the accidental bumping or proximity to others, which typically led to violence, and on the rare occasion—death.

Nick stepped up to the serving line. Unlike gen pop, meals served in D Wing were done by the guards. Everything was controlled and everything was monitored. Nick raised his beige plastic tray to chest level and began sidestepping along. No choices were given. Each compartment on the formed plastic tray was filled by the guard in front of him. Talking was not permitted. One meat, one starch, one fruit, and one dessert. At the end of the line was a clear plastic cup with water. Nick completed his stutter step routine and moved to the table he regularly occupied. Soon the only inmate he'd connected with took a seat across from him.

Sherman Wilson was taller than Nick by two inches, but his six feet four inches appeared even taller due to the man's rail thin frame. Sherman wore thick coke-bottle glasses that gave him an innocent, almost nerd-like quality. He was anything but.

In the outside world Sherman Wilson had been an enforcer for a powerful street gang with ties to founding members of the Black Panthers. Sherman had been labeled a serial killer by the Department of Justice due to the number of bodies he had under his belt. Nick knew this to be an incorrect tag. Wilson wasn't a serial killer, he was a hit man. The only reason he'd been caught was because of a person he didn't kill. The irony of which was not lost on Wilson. He had refused to kill a witness to one of his executions.

Sherman had told Nick the story in a rare moment of openness. He was on a hit. Without going into too much detail, he'd explained that another crew had moved in and was taking up some of the trade in his gang's area. Sherman delivered the message with a bullet to the back of the dealer's head. A twelve-year-old girl on a back-porch landing had seen him carrying out one of his assignments. He saw her too, but refused to put a bullet in her.

The girl later positively identified him out of a lineup and bravely testified to it during the trial. Sherman said he respected the girl's strength of character and accepted his fate. The gang, however, did not, and Sherman found out his replacement had sent a message to the neighborhood by killing the girl and her grandmother. That was the last time Sherman Wilson claimed any affiliation to the gang.

It was because of Sherman's moral code Nick had come to trust the man. That and the fact that Sherman had stepped in and stopped a brutal attack on Nick when he'd first arrived at D Wing.

Word had quickly spread to the residents of D Wing that an FBI agent had joined their ranks. Most of the convictions served had been done so at the hands of a federal investigation, so the chance to take their pound of flesh was a top priority for some. Three inmates had conspired against Nick. The attack was fast and brutal. Nick had been struck from all sides simultaneously. The blows were well aimed and delivered with devastating effectiveness. One inmate snapped his tray in half and was attempting to slit Nick's throat with the jagged edge. That's when Sherman Wilson demonstrated his own set of skills. He moved through all three men, stepping on knees and manipulating elbows and wrists. The crunch of their snapped limbs was sickening. All three were hospitalized and never returned to D Wing.

Nick had asked him why he helped him, and Sherman had simply said, "It was the right thing to do."

6

"You're looking a little sweatier than usual today," Sherman said as he slipped into the chair in front of Nick.

"And you're looking a little thinner, Sherm," Nick said, giving a slight grin.

Sherman laughed. "If you're going to start pitching your inner warrior crap I'm going to get up and go sit with fat Culver."

Nick looked over toward Culver to make sure he hadn't heard the jibe. The large killer always sat alone. The rolls of his neck fat jostled as he devoured the food on his tray. Nick often wondered how the man continued to gain weight under these conditions. It was like watching those post-apocalyptic shows in which soft actors and actresses play survivalists. Satisfied Sherman hadn't offended Culver, Nick turned back to his friend.

"So, what's on the agenda today?" Sherman asked with a chuckle.

"Always a toss-up. So many options," Nick said.

"Maybe it's time," Sherman prodded.

"Don't start with me. Save your psychobabble for someone else."

"It's not psychobabble Nick. You need to get some closure so you can move forward."

"Closure? I closed that chapter of my life almost a year ago," Nick said, breaking eye contact.

"If you won't allow her to visit then the least you can do is write her a letter," Sherman said.

Nick looked back at Sherman, who stared unblinkingly back through the coke-bottle glasses, the size of his eyes amplified. It was like those lenses gave him some supernatural ability to peer deep into Nick's soul and he hated it.

"I regret telling you about her," Nick muttered.

"I'm glad you did. It made me feel a whole lot better about saving your cracker ass."

Nick laughed. It was a strange world he now lived in where the gangly, racially charged ex-hit man provided him with his only sense of humanity.

Nick had banned all visitors after his final relocation to Masterson Correctional. Anaya had sent several requests, but he denied them. He couldn't face her. He couldn't bear to see the disappointment in her eyes. His past decisions had come back to haunt him, and it had cost him everything to include his unborn child—their unborn child. He'd faced no greater failure in his life.

Declan had also tried to use his swagger with the Bureau to arrange a sit down, but, as was legally Nick's right as an inmate, he could refuse any unwanted contact. Nick had taken his new assignment as a resident of D Wing seriously and knew he would be unable to psychologically survive the remaining years of his life if he maintained his previous connection to the outside world. So, he severed it, completely isolating himself to the recesses of D Wing and his new inner circle of Sherman Wilson.

The great warrior philosopher, Sun Tzu, gave him wisdom.

The ability to gain victory by changing and adapting according to the opponent is called genius.

7

He watched as she got off the bus. The light blue scrubs were wrinkled, her bun had come loose, and her thick black curls spiraled out. An indication the shift she'd just completed was not an easy one. She was a certified nursing assistant, CNA, at a local hospital. She picked up as many shifts as she could, but living in Connecticut was not easy on her salary.

Watching her meander toward her apartment building, he knew this was just one part of her very busy day. Only a few hours' reprieve before she'd be back on another bus heading to her second job. Most people would spend the interim sleeping, but not Shakira Anderson. She would be taking the block of time to spend quality time with her toddler, Jamal Jr. He watched her as she walked along the row of brownstone buildings, long-since converted from single family homes of the fifties into apartments mishandled and run by slum lords. It was a dangerous neighborhood. He knew this first hand. Its streets were familiar and so was the criminal element plaguing them.

Shakira paid no mind as she passed by his car, walking in a half daze of exhaustion. The grind of life had aged the woman beyond her twenty-six years of life. Declan watched her with a combination of deeply rooted guilt and unabashed reverence. His decision to shoot Jamal Anderson, nearly two years ago, had left her without a husband and her son without a father. The money he'd anonymously bestowed upon her had been tucked away into a savings plan for her son. He knew this and was glad it would benefit him in the distant future. But as he watched the condition of her life, he wondered what future would her son have growing up here? Declan wished that she had used a percentage of the sixty thousand to move into a better neighborhood and decided he would contact the attorney to free up some of the money to do just that.

Declan checked in on her from time to time. It was some sort of penance he'd created, forcing himself to bear witness to the unforeseeable consequence of his split-second life and death decisions. It was Declan Enright's twisted form of self-help therapy. His wife, a licensed Psychologist, had warned him of the damage this would do to him. But Declan was as stubborn as he was brave. She knew it and had long ago caved on this front.

He racked his brain to come up with an additional solution to alleviate his tortured soul. Deep down he knew nothing would ever completely resolve the void created when taking another's life. He'd done this numerous times in his previous life while serving among the Navy's elite SEAL Teams, but warfare is its own burden and Declan managed to shoulder the weight better than most. Taking a life as a cop had a much more intimate feel, personalizing its aftermath. And so here he sat, taking in the sight of Jamal's widow, making his ritualistic atonement.

Shakira moved along the rows of concrete steps, one of which was occupied by several men in their late teens or early twenties. A couple cat calls rang out as she moved past. He watched her ignore the banter, keeping her head down and pressing forward. Apparently, this did not sit well with one of the men. He stood up, throwing his hands in the air in dramatic fashion. The rear of his jeans sagged, exposing a pair of purple polka-dot boxer briefs. A bulge in his front waistline concealed by the partially tucked shirt indicated he was most likely carrying a gun. Declan opened his door as he heard him yell, "Bitch, I said I'm talking to you!"

Shakira kept stride but looked back. Fear flashed across her eyes, but Declan watched as she tried desperately to hide it.

The man hopped down two steps to the sidewalk and threw his hands out wide and gestured toward his crotch. "Get your big ass back here!"

Shakira's pace quickened as the goon's two minions stood up, joining him on the sidewalk. All three now trailed behind the woman, closing the gap. Declan silently slipped in behind the trio, maintaining pace but staying several feet back. They didn't notice his uninvited arrival to this party. *Why would they?* He thought. Declan spent the better part of his adult life as a ghost, operating in units that were built around the ability to move without detection. It was one of many trademark skills he possessed.

"Yo! You didn't hear my boy? He said to bring it back!" A fat counterpart said.

Shakira broke into a slight jog as she approached the front steps of her building. She reached into her purse as she ran, rummaging for her keys while bounding up the steps. She got the door open and slipped inside.

She pulled hard in an effort to close it behind her, but the saggy-bottomed thug wedged his foot between the frame and the door before it shut completely. Shakira held the interior door handle in a futile effort to stop the trio from entering. The door was ripped open and her hand came free. She fell backward to the foyer floor and screamed. She scurried back like a crab, scrambling to escape.

The three men entered, focusing on the woman on the floor before them. Shakira Anderson rolled to the side and began scrampering to her feet just as one of the men kicked her legs out from under her. The fat one licked his lips overtly as if he was preparing to feast.

"I like a girl with a little fight in 'er," the one with the polka-dotted boxers said. "Take her to the basement."

The fat thug grabbed her by the ankles and pulled hard, spinning her toward the adjacent stairwell. It was dark and the super had failed to change the bulb months ago. Shakira screamed again, attempting to get the attention of one of the neighbors. In an area like this people typically did not get involved. Especially if the troublemakers were gang affiliated. The repercussions could be deadly. No doors opened. No do-gooder exited the safety of their apartment to render aid.

During the commotion, no one had noticed Declan slip in behind the three men huddled over their prey. He said nothing as he set to work.

He'd sized up all three men while he was following behind them. The biggest known threat was the skinny kid with the gun and he needed to be dealt with first.

Declan kicked hard at the back of Polka Dot's left knee and simultaneously pulled him backward by the shoulders. The unsuspecting man toppled easily back to the hard tile of the entranceway. Declan dropped his right knee hard on his neck, driving the man's face into the flooring. He was dazed almost to the point of unconsciousness, and Declan seized this opportunity to rip the gun from his waistline. The man relented under the weight of Declan's knee. With the gun in hand Declan drove the butt of the small caliber pistol down on the struggling man's temple, rendering him completely unconscious.

The man that had been standing next to Mr. Saggy Pants turned, trying to make sense of the last few seconds of madness. As he turned, Declan launched at him, crashing his elbow hard into the man's face. The blow sent him back into the row of metal mailboxes affixed to the opposite wall. The combination of impacts was devastating, and the man slid down the wall and slumped on the floor. A trail of blood smeared the wall, leaking from the back of the man's head. His eyelids fluttered rapidly and his eyes rolled to the back of his head, indicating he was temporarily out of the fight.

The fat man, seeing Declan's assault, had released Shakira's ankles, and his right hand was moving quickly toward his waist. Declan saw the glint of a large knife. Declan reacted, throwing the gun in his hand at the man's face. The fast-moving hunk of steel found its mark striking the man between the eyes, instantly breaking his nose. The introduction of pain and flow of blood caused the fat man to drop the knife and the blade clanked loudly against the tile.

The fat man was stunned and his head arced back. He gripped his nose with two hands, the blood poured out through the gaps between his fingers. His large body teetered momentarily before yielding to the force of the assault. The man staggered back, losing his footing at the edge of the basement stairwell. He fell down the same flight of stairs he'd tried to take Shakira Anderson down. He lay upside down and unmoving in a heap at the bottom.

Declan outstretched his hand. Shakira took it with a look of utter bewilderment. He gently brought the woman to her feet. "It's okay. You're safe now."

"Thank you," Shakira said softly, surveying the three men in various states of incapacitation.

"I think you better head to your apartment and I'll get this cleaned up," Declan said, scanning the three downed men.

"How can I repay you?" Shakira asked gratefully.

"Move."

"Move?" She asked.

"It's not a safe place for you. And definitely not after this. You'll be receiving some money in a few days to get you a better situation. Until then do you have somewhere to stay?" Declan asked.

"Money? A place to stay? Uh... yes," Shakira rambled, understandably overwhelmed.

A soft groan ebbed out of the fat man at the bottom of the stairs. Declan shot her a look. "Time for you to go."

Shakira nodded and scurried down the hall toward the stairwell leading to her second floor apartment.

Declan quickly went about retrieving the gun and knife from the floor and searching the thugs more thoroughly to make sure there weren't any other weapons. He used their shoelaces to hog tie the three. A good Navy man can always pull off some knots. Especially when you're trained to do it holding your breath for two minutes while submerged twenty meters below surface.

He didn't want to try to explain in great detail to the local cops what he was doing in the neighborhood, so he used the fat one's cellphone to call the police. He gave a loose interpretation of what was going on and what crime was being committed at the time of his citizen's arrest.

He opened the door to leave. Before departing he turned to the three men who were now conscious but tightly bound. "If you ever bother that woman again, I'll come back. And next time I won't be so nice."

Declan slipped out of the door and walked back toward his Bureau-issued sedan parked several buildings away. A lean man, clean-cut with a slight gray along his temples, was leaning casually against the passenger side door.

"Hey friend, you're leaning on my car," Declan said nonchalantly as he got closer.

"I know," the man said.

"Whatever you're selling, I ain't buying," Declan said. His cavalier tone flashed to impatience.

"You really are a shit magnet."

"Not sure what you're talking about," Declan said, sliding his hand close to the Glock 23 subcompact holstered inside the rear right side of his waistline.

"Easy Declan. No need for that," the man said.

"Do I know you?" Declan said, his hand unmoved.

"Not by face, but by name."

Declan eyed the man cautiously but said nothing.

"I'm Jay. I felt like it was time for you and I to meet face-to-face."

"How do I know you are who you say you are?" Declan said, knowing the need to vet everything.

"I called you a while back using your wife's number to contact you."

Declan moved his hand away from his gun and relaxed slightly, but not completely. When a CIA spook appeared out of nowhere, it carried with it an inherent level of danger. "So, why now? Why here?"

"It's complicated," Jay said.

"It always is," Declan mumbled.

"We need to talk."

"Okay. So talk," Declan said.

"Not here. I have a car waiting," Jay said, gesturing to a heavily tinted SUV parked down the street.

"What about my car?"

"I've got someone to drive it back to headquarters for you," Jay said.

"Is this the part where you tell me I've got no choice?" Declan said, raising an eyebrow.

"We've always got choices. This is a one-time offer and I'd like you in on it," Jay said matter-of-factly with no hint of a veiled threat. "Take it or leave it."

Declan sighed. "Nick trusted you. So, by default I do too."

"It's funny you said that."

"Why?" Declan asked, cocking his head.

"Because Nick's the reason I wanted to talk to you."

Declan tossed his keys to a thick-necked, ruddy-faced man who said nothing as he exited the rear of the SUV and walked toward Declan's sedan.

8

The news was playing out on a flat screen television hanging from the wall. Each channel carried the same story and similar images. The security footage had been leaked, as was the plan, and the black and white image played out in forty-two inches of high definition quality. Students were running as the gunman began firing randomly into the crowd. It was pandemonium, all captured on tape. Then came the explosion like a visual exclamation point, driving home the tragedy with devastating effect to the millions of viewers around the world. The camera flashed into a bright white and then faded to black, returning to the panel of experts prepared with canned responses.

The live feed was from the outside of Connerton-Jacobs High School, playing in the backdrop while politicians and former federal agents weighed in with their two cents. This was typical of these events and had become the staple of every news junkie's day, giving them their dose of terrible tragedy. The mental recovery from seeing images and scenes like the one depicted was starting to have minimal impact. Viewers became desensitized as violent extremism had begun to occur more frequently.

The repeated videos on a loop showed students and teachers

running. Police, Fire, and EMS converging and triaging the victims. Tearful cries of anguish as groups of survivors were surrounded by supporters. Vigils were held and memorabilia covered the makeshift shrines signifying the tragic end of innocent lives. Then came the interviews of the traumatized as victims came forward to share their moments of horror.

A press conference had been announced where answers were promised to be given. Local authorities and community leaders banded together in a unified visual front. The President would make a public address condemning this act and others like it. All of it had been done before. All of it would be done again. And with little, if any, effect.

The group seated in the conference room watched and listened, absorbing the devastation played out before them.

"Twelve dead and twenty-nine wounded," Tanner Morris's voice grumbled, interrupting the newscaster's synopsis. "And what do we think of this?"

The room was silent, except for the shifting of chairs as the people seated around the hand carved mahogany table turned to face the man. Each person seated at the table managed equally important roles in the organization, but the man at the head, Tanner Morris, was on a totally different tier. One of the most unique rise-and-fall-and-rise-again stories in Fortune-500 history. Tanner had designed multiple successful startups, dabbling in a variety of markets. For a man who grew up in the blue-collar Midwest as a mechanic's son, he'd gone on to amass a small fortune. He did it all without ever attending college. Technically he never completed high school, but he did earn his GED.

Tanner Morris hit his first million before the age of nineteen. Things seemed to come together with relative ease until tragedy derailed his path.

Tanner's daughter Wendy, the youngest of his two children, committed suicide. It wrecked him—his life became a collision course of drugs and alcohol. One night he crashed his car, killing three people when he crossed into oncoming traffic and hit another vehicle head on. He served five years for the vehicular manslaughter. It had been a hard five years, but he rebuilt his empire. Although his focus had drastically changed.

The images flashing across the now-muted television screen were a result of his brainchild.

He knew no one at the table would dare to assess this first test run. At the end of the day, only he could weigh in on the success or failure of the operation. No one spoke. The assessment was being weighed, evident by the lines squiggling across his furrowed brow. Tanner Morris could easily be mistaken for a banker if it wasn't for the blue ink of the tattoo stretched on the side of his neck, a little memento from his prison affiliation with the Brotherhood. He was not a white supremacist nor did he hold their beliefs, but when caged with dangerous men survival was key.

"Did our test run equal a success?" Morris asked again, demanding a response.

All of the others in the room nodded solemnly.

"I agree. And you think that we are ready to widen the scope of our operation?" Morris asked gruffly.

The four members of his counsel spaced around the ornate table each shot quick glances at one another, a weak effort to decide who should answer. The eyes of the others locked on the small-statured floppy-haired technician, Simon Belfort. He looked like he'd be more comfortable surfing a wave in Hawaii or serving someone a latte as a barista. But one thing was for certain, Belfort was a tech genius. He'd proven that time and again on various assignments. Belfort was also loyal, and for those reasons Tanner Morris hand picked him to run the technical aspects of this endeavor.

"I—I say yes. We're ready. Analysis of the statistics point in that direction. Several Prospects are in the queue," Belfort squeaked. He desperately shuffled the stack of paper in front of him looking through his data, searching for the answer to the question that was sure to follow.

"Several is not a number. I need a number. Quantifiable data has numbers not generalities," Morris said calmly. But everyone in the room knew that lying just beneath the surface was a percolating rage. The group had learned to watch for the telltale sign Morris was about to launch into one of his legendary emotional eruptions. The veins alongside his neck would bulge and his face would redden.

Belfort cast a quick glance, looking up from his paperwork, and his tension eased a bit, seeing Morris's face was still calm. The early warning alarm of a tempestuous outburst had not been triggered.

Finding the sheet he was looking for, Belfort sat up and cleared his throat. "Sorry about that, Mr. Morris. As of this morning we have locked in on thirty-one prospects from seventeen different states. I've got over one hundred and sixty-two potentials who are closing in on the challenge stage."

"What is the percentage of people who reach the challenge stage that move on to prospect level?" Morris asked.

"We've seen an improvement in the percentile as of last week with forty-eight percent moving forward into prospect status. That's up sixteen percent," Belfort said pridefully and equally relieved to be able to deliver the answer with stats.

Morris nodded. "That brings me to my next question. Where do we sit financially?"

No one needed to look around the room as to who would answer this question because there was only one who handled this aspect of the company. Sarah Barnes, the company's chief financial advisor, tapped her iPad and the pale light of her device's screen illuminated her pockmarked face. What she lacked in beauty she made up tenfold in brains. "Our profits remain steady

and we stand at one point two million for last quarter. I project we will exceed that during these next few months based on the last few weeks."

"I need Prospects in all fifty states. A Prospect is only a high-potential candidate. Our ultimate goal is to get them through to the Patriot level. Is that clear?" Morris eyed each and every member of his council, stopping at Graham Morris, his son. "Graham, you need to up your game son. I must have those Prospects turned into Patriots. Can I count on you?"

"Of course," Graham said coldly.

Graham, who'd been extremely gifted as a child, graduating high school at fifteen and college by nineteen, had also demonstrated a rare talent for the psychological manipulation of others. Tanner Morris had tested the limits of his son's ability and was very pleased with the end result. Facing a brutal and costly divorce, Tanner deployed his only living child to exploit the weakness of his soon-to-be ex-wife.

Graham spent months subliminally implanting thoughts into his mother, a woman he despised. She wasn't mean or cruel. Those traits would have been understood by Graham. He hated the woman because above all other things she was weak. Graham had found a penchant for hurting the weak. It started with an injured squirrel he'd found when he was six. Dispatching the creature through slow torture, the experience was one of his formative memories and he recalled it fondly to this day.

His father had caught him on occasion during one of his experiments, usually with a neighbor's cat or dog. He preferred cats because of the sound they made. Tanner Morris had turned a blind eye to his son's predilection, enabling his drive.

Graham deployed a barrage of psychological attacks on his mother. She didn't love him anyway. He saw the way she looked at him. It was far from the reverence she held for his sister Wendy. Two weeks after Graham began his social experiment with his mother, Alice Morris committed suicide. He'd realized he derived an immense pleasure from this new technique for exploring his deviance. Like his first squirrel, his mother's death had been a cherished and life changing experience.

After destroying his mother's life, the bond between Graham and his father had been unbreakable.

Graham had been tasked with shaping Prospects. He'd only test run one Prospect and taken him all the way to Patriot status. The methodology Graham had deployed proved to be effective. The news of Sasquatch_187's deployment had been a marked success and was relatively easy. He looked up at the scene on the television and smiled at the outcome of his latest experiment.

"How much time?" Morris asked.

"Tough to say, but now that we have proof positive on the approach, then I'd say we might have your fifty Patriots within two weeks," Graham said confidently.

"Alright," Tanner said giving a dismissive wave of his hand. "That's it for now."

The group stood and filed toward the ornate door of the small conference room. "Tank, stay for a moment," Tanner Morris said to the large man.

Thomas "Tank" Jones was the only member who couldn't pass for anything but a dangerous ex-military type. His stout five-foot, six-inch frame was packed with more muscle and tattoos than seemed humanly possible. The high and tight haircut coupled with his sun damaged skin added an element of ruggedness. The intensity of his look was exacerbated by a large scar stretching across the left side of his face that stopped at his ear. The top third of that ear was missing, lost on some distant battlefield.

"Yes?" Tank asked. His voice a rasp from years of yelling and chain smoking.

"He's still alive?" Morris asked.

"He is. From what the news accounts are saying... yes."

"We need to rectify that," Morris said, drumming his fingers on the varnish coating the wood conference table. "We can't have him talking about the game. There can be no exposure until we make the announcement. And there can be no link to us."

"Consider it done." Tank nodded, turned, and walked out of the room. A man of little words, but deadly efficiency. Tanner Morris never micromanaged him, giving Tank free reign to accomplish each task with minimal oversight.

Tank smiled as he walked out of the room. Having a new mission, regardless of its purpose or target, gave him great satisfaction.

9

Nick pressed his hands on the wall and heard the door's release. The days blurred into one repetitious cycle. Every time the lights came on it was like someone hit the reset button on his life.

Excellence consists in breaking the enemy's resistance without fighting. He'd read those words too many times to count and it reminded him to fight back. Resist being swallowed by the darkness, he told himself. Nick wouldn't allow himself to concede to the tedious weight of his circumstances.

He'd pushed himself extra hard during his pre-lunch workout and his palms were moist with sweat, barely maintaining their purchase on the smooth gray acrylic paint of his cell's wall. *Inmates, turn and face the open door,* the voice on the PA commanded. The familiar pause before the next static-etched command sounded, *Keep your hands at your side and exit your cell.*

Nick stepped out of his cell and onto the landing as he'd done two hundred and ninety-seven times since being relocated to Masterson Correctional. His poorly constructed sneakers and faded orange jumpsuit were the extent of his worldly belongings.

Nick stood on the yellow painted line centered on the four-foot stretch of the landing. The railing running along the balcony had five horizontal bars spaced at one-and-a-half-foot intervals, bringing the height to seven and a half feet, a little over a foot above Nick's six-foot-two stature. It was done to prevent the potential of an inmate being tossed to the lunch and recreation area below. No one had attempted such a feat in the short time since Nick had taken up residency, but Sherman had said the bars weren't always as high. The implication needed no further explanation.

Face inward and maintain your interval. The last of the announcements given for a while—until the lunch hour ended and they'd be returned to their cages. It was surreal for Nick to see himself among this population. He'd spent the better part of his life hunting men like these and now he ate beside them. He pushed the thought from his head. Nothing good would come from dwelling on a past he couldn't change.

Tray in hand, Nick began his side step shuffle along the chow line. The guard gave a moment's pause before manipulating the tongs to retrieve a slab of gray meat. Something was off. Maybe it was the way he looked at him or the extra careful nature in which the guard selected his food. But one thing Nick Lawrence excelled at was his ability to read people, and he trusted his instincts above all else.

"Make sure you take time to digest your steak," the guard said, breaking the cardinal rule of no communication.

The comment caught Nick off guard but he said nothing in response. Nick continued moving down the line, as he'd always done, until his tray was full. He stepped away from the chow line and the guard, moving toward his table. Sherman Wilson would be joining him shortly.

Nick tore at the meat with his hands. No knives, plastic or otherwise, in the D Wing. The flimsy spork was the only permitted eating tool and the guards inspected each inmates' plate and utensil before disposal to ensure that none of the small plastic points had been broken off. A prisoner's ingenuity was an amazing thing, especially when he was interested in killing another.

So, Nick abandoned the spork and used his fingers, separating the meat into several pieces. The jailhouse version of Salisbury steak came apart easier than a normal cut of beef and the piece Nick held was flimsier than most—he immediately saw the reason why.

A bit of plastic was lodged in the center of the beef. It was the size of a pack of sugar. Nick quickly took a big bite of the meat, shoving the plastic into his mouth with it just as Sherman dropped into his seat. The watery juices trickled across his hand.

"Well, you sure are hungry today. All those push-ups you do increases your appetite," Sherman said. The former hit man cracked a wide smile, exposing the bright white of his teeth.

Nick nodded and tried to smile back while chewing. His tongue manipulated the piece of plastic into the space on the right side of his mouth between his teeth and cheek. Nick swallowed the meat, being careful not to accidentally ingest the item.

"Nothing like Salisbury steak. It must be Tuesday. Or Wednesday? Maybe Saturday?" Nick said, reciting a joke they'd used more times than he cared to admit. Somehow to them it always proved a source of entertainment and Sherman chuckled.

10

The remainder of the lunch hour had passed without much fanfare. Nick returned to his cell and waited until the heavy steel of his door closed. The door had a small vertical window, six inches wide and one foot high. The pane of glass was heavy and was used for the guards' random visual inspection of the cells. There was no way to communicate with other prisoners, not that Nick wanted to. In other installations inmates created their own form of Morse code, banging on pipes or walls. They used mirrors angled out of the bars to eyeball others, lip reading words unspoken. Not in D Wing. The walls were thick and the space between each cell had an additional layer of soundproofing. There was no exposed piping near the sink and toilet.

The silence actually turned out to be one of Nick's favorite aspects of his time at Masterson. He was grateful he didn't have to hear the constant whine of attention-seeking jailbirds. In those twenty-two hours of isolation, Nick Lawrence explored the depths of his mind, searching for answers that had long since eluded him.

Nick put his hands to his mouth and coughed loudly. His left hand now contained the small piece of plastic. He stood and retrieved The Art of War from his bookshelf. *Is it a book shelf if it only contains one book?* Nick pondered as he looked at the now-empty shelf. These ridiculous questions had become more common as the days of isolation stacked up. He'd found he could lose hours to his conundrums. But when your life is suspended in a timeless void, those hours hold no value.

He opened the book and placed the thin piece of plastic between the pages. Nick turned his back to his cell door, concealing his actions from view of any passing guard. Upon examination, Nick noticed the plastic was a vacuum sealed pouch. Looking closer, he could see it was a tightly folded bit of paper.

Satisfied no guard could see, Nick removed the plastic square, bringing it to his mouth. He used his teeth to gnaw at the packaging, tearing at the grooved edge. It took a couple of failed attempts before getting the corner to separate. Nick pinched and twisted at the small opening with his fingers. The airtight seal released and the plastic loosened. He was careful not to rip the contents. Someone had obviously gone through a great deal of trouble to get this to him and he was intrigued. Nick tapped the folded paper into the seam of the book and looked over his shoulder, ensuring a guard wasn't peering into his cage.

He understood the implications of the discovery of any potential contraband during a random inspection, so Nick slipped the plastic wrapping into his mouth and swallowed hard. The rough edges scratched at his throat as he worked it down. He set the book down which now held the mysterious note and moved over to the sink. Nick pumped the handle down three times, creating a trickle from the faucet. Cupping his hands, he filled them with the tepid water and hastily slurped at it. He gagged once as he pushed the contents down his esophagus.

Clearing his throat, Nick returned to the book on his bed and opened it back up to the page containing the note.

He unfolded the thin white paper and stared at the hand-written words.

. . .

Nick,

You need to accept Declan's request to speak with you. He's already filed the contact order. You need to hear what he has to say. I'd be dead long ago if it wasn't for you. Time to repay my debt.

Jay

Nick sat back in deep thought, pondering the message. He then tore the note into small pieces, forcing each one into his mouth. He swallowed hard, his saliva did the work of disintegrating the paper, making it easier to get down than the plastic.

He looked at the open book. Sun Tzu's words taunted him. *Opportunities multiply as they are seized.*

Nick closed the book. His decision had been made.

11

Tank sat outside of Jessup County Memorial Hospital and watched as the media circus frothed at the hopes of an exclusive interview or candid shot from one of the shooter's family members. This was not the hospital where the critical victims of Sheldon Price's shooting were being cared for. The severely injured students were transported and treated at Vanderbilt University Medical Center. It was the closest Level I trauma center in the Volunteer State to the incident.

The media had initially flooded the victims in recovery, but the wave of media interest had receded in the last few days, shifting focus to the possible recovery of the killer. The world was apparently more interested in the mind of such a person than the survivors' plight.

His blood boiled as he watched the activists parading around the media vans with their hand-painted signs calling for second amendment reform. Every shooting brought forth this group of fanatics. He liked guns and appreciated his right to carry one.

Tank breathed deeply and calmed himself by thinking of the brutality he'd just unleashed on Doctor Gray. Violence always centered him.

Tank had been surveying the hospital for the last six hours, patiently waiting for his opportunity. Dr. Gray had exited the south side of the medical facility, avoiding the media cameras. He was roughly Tank's size, albeit the good doctor's thickness came in the way of fat. It had been a relatively easy thing, killing the physician. Tank found it to be a far easier thing than most people realized. He was glad more didn't understand its simplicity because it lessened the competition for gainful employment.

A tap of the doctor's bumper on a stretch of roadway with no traffic. The pudgy doctor had exited to examine the damage to the rear bumper of his Prius. Tank fired his silenced pistol twice into the back of his head and stuffed the body into the trunk of his rental, rented under a name and license that didn't exist. Tank didn't need to kill the doctor. He could have just as easily rendered him unconscious and left him tied up. *But what's the fun in that?* He only needed the doctor's identification and security badge to navigate the increased security surrounding Sheldon Price. And now he had them.

For a reason only known to him, Tank felt more composed and relaxed after a kill than at any other time. He truly believed he was the reincarnate of some great warrior and the only way to bring balance to his psyche was to satiate his bloodlust. In a rare moment of unguarded conversation he'd revealed this to the woman he loved. She laughed. She was now dead too. And afterward Tank never shared his private thoughts again.

12

Tank clipped the doctor's credentials to the white lab coat and moved toward the hospital's south entrance. A crisp breeze whipped across the parking lot and the cold air cut through the thin green scrubs he was wearing under the coat. He felt naked and wondered how doctors and nurses spent their days wearing this thin pajama-like material. Tank refocused himself, entering the building through the same doors the now deceased Dr. Gray had exited less than an hour before.

Tank knew his unique scars might catch the attention of others, so he affixed a light green surgical scrub cap, masking most of his damaged face and ear. He carried a thick file folder on a clipboard he'd swiped from a nursing station as he passed by a distracted medic talking with an attractive young nurse. Tank moved quickly and it gave him an air of importance, not making eye contact with any staff he passed. Doctor Gray's credentials were flipped to avoid being detected by a known associate.

He stood by the elevator located away from the main lobby area and pretended to be intently reading the file before him. Two orderlies had already pressed the up button and paid no attention to Tank. Doctors and nurses were commonplace in a hospital. Not too difficult to blend.

"My opinion, they should let the bastard die," one of the orderlies said. Noticing Tank lingering behind them, he looked over his shoulder at Tank. "What do you think doc?"

"I'm actually on my way up to see the little bastard right now," Tank said with a smile.

The orderlies laughed at Tank's affirmation. His snide comment resonated with the two orderlies, and by the simplest of manipulations he'd garnered their respect. The doors to the elevator opened and Tank followed the two men inside.

"You said you're going to five doc?" the orderly asked.

"Yup. Time for the little bastard to get his medicine," Tank snarked.

All three men laughed.

He was glad the men had engaged him. It made locating Sheldon Price that much easier. Otherwise he'd been left to bumble his way from floor to floor, greatly risking an increased exposure.

The orderlies had exited on the third floor without a further word. Tank rode the rest of the way in silence. The elevator dinged, announcing his arrival to the fifth floor. He stepped out into the low murmur of voices and whirring mechanics of a variety of life-saving machines.

Tank took a moment to scan his surroundings. He was looking for the one thing he knew would identify Sheldon Price's room from all others—police. It wasn't long before he saw the two uniformed police officers standing guard at the far end of the floor.

His purposeful walk began again, and Tank moved past the floor's nurses' station without giving them a second look. The officers turned at his approach and seemed unconcerned. Their guard obviously lowered at Tank's ensemble.

The officer on the far side of the door remained seated. The one closest to Tank stood. Tank flashed Doctor Gray's credentials quickly and dismissively in a manner balanced between routine and annoyance. The officer seemed less than interested in examining them carefully.

"Afternoon doc. I'm going to need you to sign the log. You know the drill," the officer said flatly.

"Sure thing," Tank said with a smile as he took the clipboard from the young officer. Tank looked at the scribble of the other signatures on sheet and laughed to himself. Doctors really can't write legibly, which worked in his favor. Tank made his mark.

"Got the mask on huh?" the seated officer said inquisitively.

"Oh yeah. Got a bit of a cold. I don't want the poor boy to catch his death," Tank said with a laugh, knowing the cops would resonate with his dark sense of humor.

He'd assumed correctly as both men chuckled at the joke, and he handed the log back.

The officer pushed down on the handle, opening the door. Tank slipped inside, closing the door behind him.

13

The room was quiet, except for the beeps and buzzes from the machines bookending Sheldon Price's bed. Tank approached, examining his file folder as he closed the distance. Price stirred, groaning as he rotated his body toward him.

"Hello Sheldon, I'm Doctor Gray. How are you feeling today?" Tank said, doing his best to deliver a believable guise consistent with standard bedside manner banter.

"I'm okay I guess," Sheldon said weakly. His voice came in muffled rasps. His face was bandaged, leaving only his right eye exposed.

"We need to talk." Tank's demeanor changed and became gravely serious. Sheldon must have noticed because his one eye widened slightly.

"Okay. What about?"

"Who did you talk to?" Tank asked quietly.

"Talk to? About—what? I mean who are you?" Sheldon asked. His voice quivered.

"Who did you tell about Rebel Dogs? About Sasquatch_187? About the Patriot level?" Tank spat the questions in rapid fire succession.

"N-n-n-nobody," Sheldon stammered.

"Are you sure?"

"Nobody. Oh Jesus! Who are you?" A tear fell from Sheldon's right eye.

"I'm the last face you'll ever see," Tank said quietly, moving a razor-sharp scalpel across the boy's throat, opening the neck on the opposite side from where Tank was standing.

Tank stepped back quickly avoiding the arterial spurt. He pulled the curtain to block the view from the hallway. It would take Sheldon price approximately thirty seconds to bleed out from the wound, long enough for him to clear the floor before triggering the monitors' medical alerts. Tank moved to the door and exited.

"Hey boys, I'll be right back. I forgot something in my office. Can I grab you a cup of coffee from the lounge?" Tank said, already moving at a quick pace down the hall.

"I'll take one. Black, two sugars," the seated officer said.

"Sounds good. Black two sugars," Tank called back over his shoulder as he shuffled away.

He bypassed the elevator and pushed the door to the stairwell. As the door closed behind him, he heard an alarm sound and the automated Code Blue announcement blare over the speakers. Tank made quick work of the stairs and pushed out into the first-floor lobby. Tank crossed the shiny yellow floors leading out toward the south exit and out the same doors he'd entered less than ten minutes before.

Thomas "Tank" Jones calmly drove out of the parking lot of Jessup County Memorial Hospital as several cruisers barreled in. The sound of police sirens worked the media personnel into a crazed frenzy. Tank watched in the review mirror at the chaos he'd created. He looked down and noticed a small drop of blood in the knuckle of his right index finger.

Deeply satisfied, Tank smiled.

14

It had been eight months since Nick had set foot in the small room. Last time his lawyer had occupied the chair facing him. Nick looked at the rugged features of the man who now filled that space. It was not the face he'd expected to see after reading the note.

The two men hadn't seen each other since the day they'd shared a vodka toast to their fallen friend, Izzy Martinez. It was the same room where Nick had spent his last moments of freedom. He remembered how the taste of the Tito's had soured in his mouth when his closest friend and fellow agent had walked him out the door of that room and into the cuffs. The end result of that journey landed him here inside the confines of Masterson Federal Correctional Facility.

Nick no longer blamed his friend, but the ability to reach that resolution had taken months of contemplation. Nick had looked the other way on a bank robbery Declan had committed. He'd realized the good in the man and looked past his mistake, leaving the case unsolved. Nick had gone against everything his training and experience had taught him in making the arrest, but he owed him his life, and on the battlefield the lines are not black and white. Some of his burden had been alleviated when he learned Declan had used the money to help a devastated family, confirming in his mind he'd ultimately made the right decision.

The biggest irony was Declan now worked for the Bureau and was attached to their world-renowned Hostage Rescue Team, or HRT. Declan was an agent and Nick a convict. Life presents some strange twists of fate.

Declan had walked him out to an awaiting team of FBI agents. As reflection gave way to clarity, Nick realized his friend had done this for his benefit. Nick understood Declan feared the arrest could go badly and he didn't want Nick to get hurt or possibly killed. But beyond that, Declan Enright wanted to be by his side at Nick's darkest hour. And for those reasons he forgave his friend, holding him in the highest regard.

The bond of their friendship was strong, and the fact that his friend, sitting across from him now, had gone through these efforts one year later to meet with him proved it to be unbreakable.

Nick sat, separated by a small heavy steel table buffed to a dull glow, reflecting the soft incandescent light above. The chairs and tables were bolted down. This was more important here than anywhere else in D Wing. Nick was convinced many an inmate would've tried to hurl them at their lawyer. Any object a Masterson convict could move was considered a potential weapon and therefore the facility was filled with countermeasures.

"Jesus, look at you," Declan Enright said.

Declan's eyes widened, betraying the shock at seeing Nick's hardened exterior. Long tendrils of dark greasy hair reached his broad shoulders. The beard, thick and matted, covered his cheek bones, the long squiggly ends dipped to the middle of his throat. He looked like a lumberjack returning home from a two-month logging expedition. The last time Declan had laid eyes on him, Nick had been a clean-cut FBI investigator. Oh, how time had changed things. But one thing Nick's rough and tough exterior couldn't change – his eyes. It was a true statement that they were a window into the soul.

Nick looked his friend over. Declan Enright was ageless, frozen in time, and somehow capable of maintaining the same physical stature indicative of the Navy's elite. He looked as though he'd just dusted the Coronado sand off of his pants before strutting into this interview room. The aura of confidence beaming from him caused other men to question their virility.

"You look... the same," Nick said flatly.

"I'd ask how the food is, but apparently they're stuffing it with steroids," Declan said, chuckling softly at his own joke.

Nick stared blankly and didn't respond. He was weighing this meeting in his mind. Eight months of isolation and then a message from Jay puts his friend in front of him. It was no small task to get the note to him and so he assumed something serious was coming. Nick waited.

"Well, I can see you're not in the mood for small talk. So, let's get to the meat and potatoes of why I'm here," Declan said, leaning in.

Nick looked back toward the closed door and the back of the guard's head that was visible in the small pane of heavy glass.

"Not to worry. They can't hear anything we're saying." Declan tapped the watch on his left wrist. "This watch sends out a signal, disrupting the audio recording. Don't ask me how it works beyond that. A courtesy of our mutual friend," Declan said.

"You'll still have only a few minutes before the guards come in. Once they realize there's an issue with the recording system, they'll terminate this interview or relocate us. They don't screw around in here."

"Then let's get on with it," Declan said. The thin smile dissipated, and Declan took on a serious look.

Nick sat back, resting his hands evenly on his thighs, still quivering slightly from the exertion of his early morning workout.

"We're breaking you out."

"You've lost your goddamned mind. Impossible," Nick said.

"I wouldn't be here if it wasn't for you. I'd be the one rotting behind bars on the bank job. I would've lost everything if you hadn't helped me out. And my daughters would be growing up without a father," Declan said softly.

Hearing the word father caused Nick to twitch and his stomach knotted. He'd pushed the memory of his baby far from his mind. But hearing Declan's reference to his own children forced it to the forefront and the tragedy of losing a child. The inexplicable pain was difficult to contain, but Nick focused on the man in front of him and pushed down his sadness.

"Apparently, from what Jay's told me, he too owes you his life. He didn't go into any great detail which I guess is par for the course with a CIA spook. But he did mention you took a few bullets for him and that he would've been dead otherwise," Declan said. "Neither one of us want to leave this world without repaying our debts. And we've come up with a way to do that."

Nick shook his head. "It's impossible. I'm not going to Shawshank my way into the shitters. I'm telling you whatever cockamamie scheme you've come up with will fail. You're living in fantasy camp."

"I said the same thing, but Jay... well that guy's at the next level. You're about to find out what your friend's been up to since you last saw him." Declan paused, clearing his throat. "I will say this—your life will never be the same once we do this. Never," Declan said with a finality that Nick had rarely seen.

"I'll entertain you on this, but only because I've got a pretty open schedule today," Nick said, giving a feeble attempt at humor.

"You're going to die today."

Nick gave his friend a double take.

"I'm going to tap the tip of your shoe. It's going to transfer a small adhesive pouch. Contained inside is a pill. Don't ask me what the hell it is, because they told me and I've never heard of it. Apparently, something Jay's team has cooked up," Declan said, speaking in rapid fire succession.

"Jay's team?"

"No time to go into that now. If you're right about them cancelling the interview then we have limited time." Declan said.

Nick felt the hard impact of Declan's foot against the toe of his shoe.

Nick looked straight ahead, giving no reaction to the contact. The transfer was complete.

"You're going to take that pill and then tie your bedsheet tightly around your neck. You're going to do all of this tonight ten minutes after lights out just before the guards do their first visual room pass. We'll handle the rest," Declan said.

"What's the pill going to do?" Nick asked.

"It's effectively going to slow your heartbeat to an unrecognizable level, at least by human touch. Meaning the guards won't be able to tell. That's why the timing is essential. They need to find you right away. There's a limited window before that pill's going to have a permanent effect."

"Permanent?" Nick said.

"Like I said—leave the rest to us."

Nick swallowed hard, digesting this plan.

"Do you trust me?" Declan asked.

Nick paused and looked hard at the man before him. "Like nobody else."

"Then get ready to be reborn."

As if on cue, the door to the room opened and two guards entered. "Excuse me Agent Enright, but there is some type of issue with the recording system in this room. We are making arrangements to have you transferred down the hall to another room."

"No need. We're done here. Thank you," Declan said dismissively.

At the direction of guards, Nick stood. He shot an affirmative glance at Declan as he was quickly shackled, connecting a long chain from his cuffs on his wrists to the ones on his ankles. The metal around his ankle rubbed uncomfortably as he was guided toward the door.

Nick shuffled down the hallway bookended by the two guards.

He moved in the direction of his cell. Regardless of the success of this mission, one thing was certain, this would be Nick Lawrence's last night as an inmate of Masterson Federal Correctional Facility. Dead or free—he'd be leaving.

15

The Shelton Public Library buzzed with the murmurs from the mass of Pebble Brook High School students who'd made the short jaunt over after their school's dismissal. It was a common occurrence and most of the teens used it as hangout. This behavior was more typical during the winter months when Sand Hill Park was too cold for comfort.

For Albert Hutchins the library was an everyday routine regardless of weather or season. It wasn't a hangout for him. It was a safe haven from the outside world, a cruel and brutal place that had left him broken and dejected.

Most days he beat all the other students because he never stopped at his locker, or as he referred to it, the beating booth. Albert ensured he avoided his locker at all costs, carrying the books for every day's subjects in his oversized and extremely burdensome backpack. He would linger in his class until the hallways cleared and then make a beeline for his next class. This tactic increased his transit safety most of, but not all of the time. Any time he'd been trapped outside of the eyes and ears of the faculty it was bad, very bad, for Albert Hutchins.

At sixteen years old he had already developed a slight hunch from slogging through his day with thirty pounds of materials. His shoulders always expressed relief when he'd release the straps at the end of his day, dropping the burdensome load.

There was one computer he always sought out, isolated from the terminal hubs arranged for the more social of his classmates. His sanctuary was set back, shrouded by large bookcases containing volumes of books he had never read. Sheldon used to read and found he could lose himself inside the pages. That was until he found online gaming. It enabled him a deeper and darker escape from his pathetic reality.

He took up his seat at his terminal and slipped his headphones on, the worn pads of which effectively closed him off from the outside world as he began his transformation. A few clicks of the keyboard and Albert Hutchins was now his alter ego, Bully_Slayer#1.

Albert spent most of his after-school time as his alternate personality, sometimes finding it difficult to disconnect. Numerous times in the recent past he'd been snapped from his gaming trance at the librarian's closing announcement. It usually took Albert the ten-minute walk home before he was able to clear his mind enough to engage in human interaction, which under the circumstances of his current living conditions was less than desirable.

His foster family was better than the last. At least the father didn't pay him midnight visits. He'd lived with the Walker family since the start of high school, but never truly fit in. He was berated the moment he walked through the door as they took out their daily frustrations. He understood his place in the pecking order around the house and also knew his value. Albert Hutchins was a government stipend for the Walker family. Nothing more, nothing less.

He'd long ago stopped caring about his life or the direction it took. His immersion in online gaming alleviated some of his despondency, but only slightly. That was until he found Rebel Dogs. The game allowed him to create a world worth living in and Albert Hutchins found something he hadn't had in a very long time, a purpose. His goal when playing was to kill every bully he encountered within the gaming platform's realm.

Albert spent countless hours learning the user gamertags of his Pebble Brook classmates. He kept a secret journal listing who they were in real life and how many times in his alternative life he'd killed them in his alternate universe. The tally grew exponentially with each passing day and he reveled in his dominance.

Not too long ago he had overheard Andy Bloom, his arch-nemesis, complaining to a friend about the Bully Slayer and how he'd love to find him in real life and kick his ass. The irony is, Andy, unbeknownst to him, had on many occasions already followed through with that threat. But for every time Andy had punched, kicked, or embarrassed him, Albert had killed him in Rebel Dogs ten times over.

The game world was designed as a free-range open play format with levels of achievement earned through actions, enabling characters to gain experience points and level up. If you wanted to steal a car, you stole a car. If you wanted to be a police officer and fight crime, you went after the guy who stole the car. If you wanted to take a hammer and drive it into the head of your enemy, well—you became like Albert "the Bully Slayer" Hutchins.

Points were awarded for each achievement earned, and every once in a while the game's admins, or administrators, would install a challenge. Successful completion of such challenges would give you badges and increase your ranking. Sometimes a challenge would be something simple like seeing how many street robberies you could complete under a set time constraint. There were a wide variety of other challenges, but the one in which Albert excelled at were Savage Countdowns. During this type of challenge, Albert was rewarded for dealing as much death to the other gamers and artificial unmanned characters as he could within the time limits. Over the short span of time he'd been playing Rebel Dogs, Albert had moved up in the rankings quickly.

Once a player's ranking reached a certain number then a title would be earned. Plebe was the lowest and assigned once a profile was created. Andy Bloom was a still a Plebe. Prospect was the next level up and extremely difficult to achieve and Albert reached it two days ago. He'd been elated and wanted to share the news with someone else, but he had nobody in his life he could confide in. That was, until yesterday when Albert had logged in to his profile and saw there was a message waiting for him in his gaming inbox.

The message was from a fellow Prospect, Graham_Cracker-Hacker. Another human being had actually sent him a message. The feeling at getting such a message was overwhelming. Graham_CrackerHacker was the first person to show him any interest in his recent memory. Today, he had sat in school all day yearning for the day's end. He stared at the clock all day, watching the seconds tick by until he was free. Albert almost considered skipping school, but knew if he did the librarian wouldn't let him in. He knew this because he'd been caught doing that before. As soon as school ended, Albert dashed out the doors and now sat staring anxiously as the game loaded. His leg bounced nervously in anticipation and he was excited to see if his new friend had written him again.

The game intro complete and his profile accessed, Albert saw there was not only one message, but three. His fingers tingled with exhilaration as he accessed them.

The first: *Are you there?*

The second: *Let's play.*

The third and most interesting to Albert read: *Are you ready to go to the next level???*

Albert messaged his response: *Yes. Where are you?*

The question was not about Graham's actual physical location, but more importantly his location within the game. Gamers could pick from active campaigns or games happening in any of the variety of environments. It was easy to get lost in Rebel Dogs' vastness, but Albert knew of the popular locations that his classmates used. But Graham_CrackerHacker was not from his school and therefore he needed to find him in the virtual world.

There was a way to tap on a gamertags and geolocate another character. Once that is done a gamer can join up the other player and interact. That's how, in the past, Albert had effectively been able to spawn near his schoolmates and kill them. He could see Graham_CrackerHacker's avatar link and click on it, trying to link up. Every attempt had failed to connect. Albert felt rejected. His hopes at meeting a new friend was not working out as planned. He slumped in his seat as a message notification dinged and Graham was number one, flashing in his inbox, indicating a new message had just been received.

Graham: *Ready? Click and see.*

Albert clicked Graham's character tag, a skull and cross bones, and Bully_Slayer#1 now stood next to Graham's avatar, who was configured to look like a ninja. Once two characters were linked, the two could chat freely. This was the first time Albert was able to chat with anyone in recent memory, and he couldn't type fast enough.

Albert typed feverishly: *How are you? Thanks for connecting. How old are you? How long have you been a Prospect?*

Albert stopped after hitting send, realizing he looked desperate and possibly a bit crazy. He didn't want to scare off the first person who'd befriended him in more than a year.

Graham did not address any of the questions asked. He only

answered Albert's question with a question of his own: *Are you ready to be a Patriot?*

Albert knew there was a final level, but no matter how many kills he'd amassed or challenges he'd completed he couldn't seem to figure out how to get there. Until now.

Albert messaged: *How?*

The chat bubble above Graham's avatar pointed toward the outside of a school.

It didn't look too much different from the school he attended. Albert surveyed the virtual scene on his monitor zooming in on the autos, unmanned characters, as they filed into the school. It looked relatively boring, as if he were watching the beginning of a regular day at Pebble Brook High. Albert could tell the autos from the manually controlled avatars because the unmanned characters had no personalized name tags hovering above them.

Albert: *What's the challenge?*

Graham: *KILL 'EM ALL.*

Albert stared at the screen and his heart beat faster. Not out of nervousness, but from the sheer excitement of it all. He'd envisioned this day in real life and relished the thought of getting to play it out now. And unlike real life, he wasn't alone. Graham, his new best friend, was standing beside him.

Albert asked: *Weapons?*

Every challenge came with additional weaponry or tools.

Graham: *Check your inventory.*

Albert made a click to the satchel icon and it opened. Inside was a device, most likely a bomb, and a pistol.

Graham: *ARE YOU READY?*

Albert typed, feeling cool and powerful. *Hell to the yeah!*

Graham: *LET'S DO THIS!!!*

The timer activated and a small countdown clock populated the upper right corner of the screen, ticking down from three minutes. Bully_Slayer#1 and Graham_CrackerHacker moved in tandem toward the front doors of the school. Graham's avatar dropped behind, letting Albert take the lead as they entered.

Albert manipulated his avatar through the crowd, shoving aside the simulated students lingering in the hallway. He moved to a more population dense area. To get the highest kill ratio in the shortest amount of time he needed to strike in a place with the most students congregating. He found the perfect place to begin his assault, the cafeteria.

The Bully Slayer switched to first person point of view, or POV, knowing it's always better to kill from that perspective. He withdrew the pistol from his inventory and aimed. Albert used the keyboard to manipulate his aiming points as he began firing into the group of students.

He was good. No, he was great, placing head shots on the virtual students. The autos reacted to his shooting and began running for the doors of the cafeteria. Albert fired at them, piling bodies at each of the exits and making it impossible for the characters to leave. The simulated student body was trapped with the Bully Slayer. Like shooting fish in a barrel, he emptied the gun and reloaded several times. With every pull of the digital trigger, Albert envisioned Andy Bloom's face.

Out of bullets, he retrieved the bomb from his inventory. The doors were now blocked for him too. The countdown timer was ticking down with only a few seconds left. Albert "the Bully Slayer" tossed the bomb into the center of the café and detonated. His screen went blank.

Albert sat in silence staring at his muted reflection in the smudged blackness of the flat-screen monitor.

Then a message in bright green letters populated the screen.

PATRIOT.

Albert involuntarily held his breath as he took in the seven letters exemplifying his life's biggest achievement.

In smaller letters beneath the word came a message:

Are you ready to take it the next level? Are you ready to be a legend in the real world?

Albert Hutchins wasn't sure what that meant, but wanted this feeling to continue. He slowly and deliberately pressed each key of his simple response.

YES.

16

"Open cell 301!"

Nick heard the words but the sound filtered in like someone screaming underwater. Then without warning all sound dissipated.

"No pulse. Get him on the gurney," said Sergeant Gary Fredrickson, D Wing shift supervisor. Panic filled his voice. No supervisor wanted an inmate to die on their watch. Not a good thing for the resume, especially for someone vying for the next Lieutenant's position. "Christ! Move his ass!"

The two large guards each positioned themselves at the shoulders and feet of Nick Lawrence. They grunted their exertion, hoisting his large frame to the lowered gurney. The two medics, who'd luckily been at the facility on an unrelated matter, were able to redirect to D Wing to assist. Fredrickson looked two shades whiter than normal, which made the pasty face of the overweight man look translucent.

Fredrickson's goal was to get the inmate in the ambulance

before anyone pronounced him dead. Then it would be a medical death and not a failure of his leadership. As arbitrary a difference it may seem, Fredrickson knew those details sometimes saved careers. With only a few years left before reaching his pension he couldn't afford the fallout. The frantic federal corrections sergeant started pushing on the back of one of the medics, trying to expedite the process.

Outside the cell, Fredrickson led the way, practically jogging along the yellow line of D Wing's second tier landing with the two medics following close behind. The right front wheel of the gurney was loose and wobbled noisily as it pulled to the right, banging loudly into the rail lining the landing. The larger of the two medics, a broad-shouldered ginger-haired man in his late thirties, adjusted the cart carrying the body of Nick Lawrence and corrected the alignment of the poor-quality bed on wheels.

Sergeant Fredrickson brought the medics to the large elevator adjacent the chow line area. He'd radioed ahead and the doors were already being held open by one of the guards.

Fredrickson ensured that inmate Lawrence was properly shackled to the gurney. He advised the medics that he'd called ahead to Mercy General, only a few miles down the road, to ensure security would be standing by to take them to a secure room in the ER. The thinner medic who was now guiding the front of the gurney into the awaiting ambulance nodded.

"Not a problem. We transport inmates back and forth all the time," the thin medic said.

"Not from D Wing. We run things a bit different tonight. I would normally have a guard ride with you, but I'm short staffed on this shift. I will have someone ordered in to assist, but it will take a little bit for me to arrange that. The hospital security staff should be sufficient until that happens. Whatever you do, those cuffs do not come off him. Do you understand?" Fredrickson said.

"Understood."

The rear doors to the ambulance closed. The sally port doors of Masterson Federal Correctional Facility clanged loudly as they opened, and Fredrickson watched as the ambulance sped away toward the first of three gated checkpoints. The sirens echoed in the stillness of the night.

* * *

"Get it running. Time's running out," the large medic said, checking the IV line.

"It'll take a minute, but we should be seeing some signs of life soon," the thin medic said.

The ambulance had pulled to the side of the road and the lights and sirens were turned off as the two men worked to revive the man strapped to the gurney. The large man reached to release the shackles that were binding the inmate to the railings.

"You think that's a good idea?" the smaller man said.

"What are you scared of?"

"Um... he's a big guy. I'm not sure how he's going to react. Sometimes people don't respond well to being dead." The smaller man moved back a bit. "Go ahead, but you're in charge of wrangling him in if things go awry."

The larger red-haired man smiled, confidently. "It'd be just like wrestling a gator."

17

The silence broke like a tidal wave above his head. Without warning the absolute quiet had pitched to full volume. The tranquil darkness that, seemingly only moments before, had completely enveloped him like a fluffy blanket lifted abruptly, the shock caused him to convulse wildly. His heart beat wildly and felt as though it would jump from his chest. Nick's body trembled violently like someone staving off hypothermia.

The mask attached to his face hissed loudly, filling his lungs with cool air. He welcomed it and inhaled deeply as if taking in his very first breath.

"He's coming out. Get ready," a voice said from somewhere around him.

Nick's eyes watered at the introduction of bright white light, blurring his vision. Disoriented, he swung his head looking for the source of the voice he'd just heard. His mind reeled, trying to comprehend his current circumstance, but his thoughts were encased in a fog that wouldn't seem to lift.

"Try to relax," a different voice said. This man's speech was deeper and thicker than the other. There was a very distinct accent that accompanied the words, but the identification of it was too far from his memory.

Relax? Nick thought. *How the hell does one relax under these circumstances?*

"It takes some time to adjust to everything that's just happened to you. Death isn't an easy thing to come back from," the thick accented voice said.

Death? Nick battled with the comprehension of the comment as he closed his eyes, giving in. The recall of the events leading up to his current predicament started to filter in, but it was a disjointed account like trying to remember a dream. But with each passing minute his mental acuity returned and with it a sense of calm.

He opened his eyes again. This time his vision cleared, and he adjusted to his surroundings. Closest to him was a muscular, fair-skinned man with bright red, almost orange, hair. Nick twisted his head back, finding the source of the other voice. This man had short dark hair and was thinner than his counterpart. The thin-framed man looked athletically fit and had a serious-ness to his eyes. Nick could readily tell both were hardened men.

Nick nodded to both and exhaled, remembering the plan and now understanding their role in it. The humidity of his breath fogged the clear rubber shell of the mask, still providing him with cool oxygen.

"Welcome back. You've got an IV drip that you're going to need a little bit longer. And I recommend the oxygen stays on too. Your brain will thank me later," the large man said. "I'm Bob and my friend over there—for now, you can call him Joe."

Nick nodded, knowing it was useless to try to talk through the hiss of the mask.

"I'm going to unshackle you. Try to stay calm," Bob said. "I'd hate to have to watch you die again."

Nick wasn't quite sure if the large man was kidding and nodded his understanding.

The cuffs released. Nick only moved his hands and feet enough to clear the shackles away. He remained supine and relaxed, rubbing his wrists.

A cellphone chimed and the man called Joe answered. He listened without saying a word and then ended the call.

"They're here. Ready?" Joe asked.

"Nick, listen carefully. We've got to transfer you to another vehicle. I'm going to help you because you're going to be fairly off balance for the next hour or so while your body comes back to homeostasis. That death pill is a real bitch," Bob said with a chuckle.

Nick gave a weak thumbs up.

Seconds later the rear doors to the ambulance swung open. Nick's body fought against him and did not cooperate, making the task of propping himself up extremely challenging. His disorientation made movement harder than he imagined and he immediately realized the truth of Bob's words. *Death isn't an easy thing to come back from.*

His eyes took a moment to adjust to the darkness outside. In the wash of light pouring out from the ambulance he saw a familiar face standing there to assist in steadying him as he exited and attempted to stand.

"I thought you looked like shit the last time I saw you, but you've taken that to the next level. Death is not a good look for you, my friend," Declan said with his infamous cocky smile.

Nick grabbed Declan's shoulder with his right arm and used his left to push the oxygen tank like a crutch along the dirt-covered breakdown lane of the roadway. The man called Bob followed closely behind holding his IV bag in one hand and supporting Nick at his left elbow.

A small box truck was parked, idling only a few feet away. The short distance felt like a marathon in Nick's current physical condition.

Declan and Bob got Nick up the ramp and laid him down on the hard paneling of the box truck's rear compartment, stripping him out of his jumpsuit and throwing a blanket over his naked body.

He then watched as Declan and Bob removed a tarp covering something on the other side of the small space of the box truck's interior. Nick saw a stack of three bodies. Two of the bodies were clothed, wearing the same medical uniforms Bob and Joe had on. The third body was naked and Nick watched as Declan and Joe awkwardly slid the jumpsuit over the third body. The size of the dead man was comparable to himself.

Bob hung the IV on a hook above Nick's head and then returned to assist in hauling the three bodies out of the rear of the truck.

With the last of the bodies out, Declan closed the doors. "Sleep tight buttercup," he said, latching the door.

Nick was once again surrounded in darkness. He knew the truth behind the age-old saying that it was always darkest before the dawn.

He rested, preparing his mind for what his next dawn would bring.

18

"It's working better than I thought. And that's a hard thing for me to say, because I was pretty confident in the potential. I just didn't think it would be this easy," Graham said. "I guess there are a lot of messed up kids out there."

"So, where does that put us in terms of timing?" Tanner Morris asked his son.

"Ahead of schedule. I'd say it's time to send the message," Graham said eagerly.

Morris looked at his son, weighing his suggestion. He had contemplated the ramifications of this next and final step. In fact, he'd been obsessed over it, but now that the objective was within grasp, he hesitated. It had been six years since he'd formulated this plan. Six years since his life had been derailed and put him on this very destructive path. *How many acts of violence needed to saturate headlines before this cultural and systemic indifference was reformed?* Tanner Morris thought to himself and knew he was about to find out.

Tanner knew the type of child he'd raised. He knew his influences on the monster he'd helped create and the deviant behavior he'd fostered for his own benefit. Looking at Graham he felt no sense of fatherly pride. His son was on a preordained journey of violence, a fact Tanner had known since the day he caught him torturing the neighbor's dog. He'd covered for his nonconformity then and wielded its potency now.

His daughter, Wendy, had not been like her brother. She was the polar opposite, an angel with not a malicious bone in her body. And *they* had taken her from him. The cruelty of others had been too much for her delicate nature. The void in Tanner Morris's life created in the wake of her death was deep and dark— a ponderous gap as wide as the Grand Canyon. The ex-convict entrepreneur hoped, against all reason, his plan would fill that hole.

"I'll bring in the others. Tank should be back in town this afternoon." Tanner looked at his son and recognized the lustful spark in his eyes, a spark only satiated by death. "We'll move up the timeline and begin prep for the final phase."

"For Wendy," Graham said.

Hearing her name gave Tanner Morris pause and he closed his eyes briefly, picturing the soft round cheeks and deep blue of his daughter's eyes. He exhaled loudly, releasing the memory. "For Wendy," he said, steadying his voice and resolve for what was to come.

19

Nick heard the conversations of others. He sat up in his darkened space and looked around. The fog lifted and his body no longer had the lagged response from earlier. Whatever he had ingested to induce his simulated death had worn off.

Nick realized he was no longer on the uncomfortable floor of the box truck. The soft leather of a couch had replaced the hard wood flooring. The oxygen mask he'd been wearing when he drifted off into oblivion was now gone. Running his fingers along the outside of his left hand, Nick felt the attachment of the IV. In the dark, he traced his fingers up the rubber tubing to the depleted soft plastic of the empty bag, hanging from the thin metallic hook of an IV holder. He tore off the tape and withdrew the needle from the vein in his hand. Not a big fan of needles, Nick shook off the wave of nausea accompanying this feat. Not being able to see clearly in the dark had assisted his ability to do this without becoming overwhelmed.

His eyes, having been closed for some time, adjusted quickly to the limited lighting of the room and he was able to vaguely make out his surroundings. Using the light coming in through the space under the door, he observed a sturdy desk and high-backed leather chair rounding out the extent of furnishings, in addition to the couch Nick was seated on.

The cool of the floor seeped up through Nick's bare feet. He was still naked. The blanket he'd been covered in was now in a heap on the floor. He stood and stretched, his joints popped as he adjusted himself. On top of the desk was a pile of clothes and pair of sneakers. He dressed, surprised at how well the clothing fit, and moved toward the door. His hand rested hesitantly on the knob, knowing that when he opened it he'd be stepping into a brand new world.

Nick entered the room, shielding the light from his eyes with his hand. All talking ceased as the former FBI agent turned inmate stood in the open space of what could best be described as an operations center. A ten-person conference table was set in the middle of the room. Scattered along the walls on both sides were cubicle-styled work stations separated by gray partitions.

Six people were seated around the table and all present turned to face him. The way they sized him up and down, he felt as though he was still naked. At the table's head was a face Nick hadn't seen in several years. The man stood and smiled.

"Welcome back from the dead, my friend," Jay said, broadening his smile.

Jay walked out from behind the table and approached. Nick remained still, taking it all in, still processing the situation.

"I know this is a lot to swallow. I'm going to bring you up to speed, but first let me introduce you to the team," Jay said, closing the gap and giving Nick a hearty embrace.

"How long was I out?" Nick asked, trying to account for lost time and to get his bearings. The room he was in had no windows and therefore he had no ability to discern the time of day.

"Not too long. About ten hours," Jay said, looking down at his watch.

"Ten hours? I can't remember the last time I slept for more than four at a clip," Nick said.

"Death is an exhausting process. Plus, I think you've been long overdue for a rest," Jay said, patting Nick's back. "Sorry it took me so long to get you here."

Nick cocked his head at Jay. "Where is here?"

"All in good time. Like I said, let's meet the others," Jay said, guiding Nick forward toward a vacant seat.

Nick approached the table and took a seat nearest the only other person he trusted in the world, Declan Enright.

"Nick, let me first say you're in the company of dead men," Jay said.

Jay resumed his position at the head of the table. The person closest to Jay gave an exaggerated clearing of her throat.

Jay chuckled. "Correction, you're in the company of dead men and women. Better?"

"I think it's more politically correct to say dead people," the woman said, laughing softly at her own joke.

"I'm Barbie. I handle logistics," she said with a nod.

Nick returned the nod. She was attractive, but not in such a way that would draw too much attention. It was her air of confidence that added to her mystique. She had strawberry blond hair and light blue eyes, bordering on gray. Her jawline was taut, indicative of a high level of fitness. She sat upright like an astute student eagerly waiting to answer the teacher's next question.

Sitting to her left was the smaller man from the ambulance, the one who'd called himself Joe. He spoke next, "I know we already met. I'm Spider. I handle interrogations."

Hearing the name Spider, Nick almost laughed out loud but stopped himself when he saw the seriousness in the dark-eyed man's stare. Nick couldn't help but feel as though he'd just entered the Justice League's secret lair. He half expected Batman to walk in.

"We met earlier. I'm Gator and I run the pre-op planning," the large red-haired man said.

Nick had heard the heavy accent before but couldn't place it in his mental haze. Louisiana or somewhere close to that locale. The nickname made sense based on the man's size and vernacular.

"I don't have a cool code name. These ass-clowns call me Wizard, naming me after the '80s movie with Fred Savage. I've filed my complaint with corporate." Wizard eyeballed the group with an exaggerated glare, a joke he undoubtedly had used on more than one occasion. "I handle all computer and technical issues. In short, I'm their hacker."

"Don't sell yourself short. You're not just any hacker, you tapped into the federal reserve database and siphoned millions," Jay said, cocking an eyebrow.

"Oh yeah, that. Well, it was for a good cause," Wizard said, laughing.

"And what cause was that?" Barbie asked.

"Me," Wizard said, grinning widely. "If you can't treat yourself, then you're not living."

"Well, you're not living anymore," Gator said.

Wizard chuckled loudly. "True. It was a terrible fire."

"I'm Declan and I'm an alcoholic," Declan said with a flat monotone delivery.

The group erupted into laughter and, as if rehearsed, in unison chimed, "Hi Declan."

The sound of his friend's voice combined with the cocky wit displayed in this room full of strangers had a calming effect on Nick. The awkward tension dissipated almost instantly.

"I know this is a bit odd. But trust me when I say this—you are in the company of some of this country's most underrated and unsung heroes. What we do here is... unique," Jay said, scanning the group members. "We operate outside of the normal parameters of other governmental law enforcement agencies. In doing so, we are able to react quicker to threats and deploy tactics not acceptable under the typical policy guidelines."

"So, which agency governs you? There's always some type of oversight. Homeland? Department of Justice?" Nick asked.

"Neither," Jay said.

"Then who sanctions you?" Nick surveyed the room. "Who funds your operation? Running something like this has got to cost a pretty penny."

"That's for a later discussion. You're not asking the right question," Jay said, looking intensely into Nick's eyes.

Nick stood at the end of the table. All eyes were on him, Declan included. "Why me? Why am I here?"

"I thought you'd never ask," Jay said, breaking into a smile. "I owe you my life. A debt not easily paid. And one I take very seriously."

Nick gave a subtle nod, knowing Jay's reference and remembering their first encounter years ago in the mountains of Afghanistan. A bloody bond that only the truly battle-tested could understand.

"I couldn't let you waste away in a cell. A cell we both would be sharing if you ever spoke about the intel gathering aspect of your assault on Montrose and his goons," Jay said.

"We'd all be in a bit of trouble on that one," Wizard said.

Nick immediately realized the support Jay had provided back then was not through his CIA channels, but by this ragtag group. He looked again at the big man from the bayou. Something was familiar but initially unplaceable, and then it dawned on him. "You were at the hospital in Austin that day."

"Yup," Gator answered in his thick backwater accent. "I wondered if you'd remember."

Nick shook his head in disbelief. Gator had been the one who Jay had sent to retrieve the tracking device. And Wizard, or Wiz, must've been the one who reverse engineered it, enabling him—well, more Declan and Izzy—to save Mouse from the traffickers.

"Jesus," Nick sighed.

"I know it's a lot to take in. Especially after just coming back from your recent near-death experience," Jay said. "Take some time to process this and wrap your head around things."

Nick sank deeper into his seat.

"So, how about it?" Jay asked, expectantly.

"How about what?"

"Becoming a part of this dysfunctional family?" Jay asked, grinning.

Nick shot a glance to Declan, who returned it with a solemn nod of his head.

"I don't see why you'd need me," Nick said dismissively.

Jay unfolded his hands and leaned in, resting his elbows on the sturdy table. "For starters, I've never seen a more tenacious investigator. I'm going to give you an opportunity to apply that, without restriction, to some of the worst offenders this country has to offer. And more importantly, I know you. I know you've been battle tested, and what you're capable of doing. You operate at a totally different level, like when my life hung in the balance. When the proverbial shit hits the fan, I want you by my side."

Nick accepted the compliment with a slight bow of his head. "Well, I guess I'm dead so there really isn't a life to go back to."

"I'm going to take that as a yes," Jay said. "Now the only thing left is to name you."

There was a murmur from the group as they began to voice their ideas. One voice, clear and louder than the others, dominated. "Wolf," Declan said. "I mean look at him. It's either that or Shaggy Dog."

"I like it," Jay said. "Wolf it is."

"Jesus, even the new guy gets a better nickname," Wizard whined.

"Meeting adjourned. We need to check the chatter and I want an update on progress with The Seven's last meeting location."

The group rose and the members dispersed to their cubicles. Declan walked over to Nick and clasped a strong hand on his shoulder. "Crazy stuff, huh?"

"That's the understatement of a lifetime." Nick gave a smile, but it came out flat. "Did I hear Jay correctly? He said The Seven. Are we talking about the same group Khaled worked for?"

"Yup, the one and only," Declan said. "Ever wonder how terror groups disappear from the headlines? Apparently, this group is the answer."

"No nickname for you?" Nick asked with cock of his head.

"I have one. The same one I used back in my days as an operator," Declan said in his typical swagger. "They call me Ace."

Nick remembered Declan's old call sign from his days in the Navy's most elite ghost unit, Alpha One. "What about Val and the girls?" Nick asked, genuinely concerned that this new position would compromise the devoted family man's home life.

"I'm not dead if that's what you're asking. Jay saw no need to fake my death. He knew me well enough to know there'd be no way I'd volunteer for this under those parameters." Declan continued, "Jay actually, through channels unknown, got the Bureau to officially reassign me on a temporary loan from HRT to a specialized security detail. It's beneficial having someone in this unit who can operate in an official governmental capacity if and when the situation dictates." Declan flashed his badge, clipped at his hip.

The hum of work filled the strange office space as the others set about their tasks. Nick surveyed his new world, a world where he was no longer Nick Lawrence.

He was now the Wolf.

20

The man pulled hard at the cigarette in balance between his fingers. In the quiet of the car he could hear the crackle of the tobacco as it burned. He'd been sitting down the street from the house for several long hours. The package arrived forty-five minutes ago and he could see the soft brown wrapping of the nondescript rectangular box occupying a portion of Debbie Johnson's tattered welcome mat.

Debbie Johnson no longer lived there and had vacated the residence months ago, at the conclusion of an extensive eviction process. The details of her life meant little to the man other than it provided a temporary usable address. His job was to select locations unlikely to draw suspicion so that deliveries could be made and picked up without notice. It was a seemingly simple task, but one filled with potential disaster. With several of the other cells neutralized, his role had become increasingly more important to his employer's cause.

He'd been hand-picked for a new and more important role. The group's reclusive leader had reached out to him directly. Receiving the call had been the equivalent of speaking to Allah himself. He remembered the coldness of his voice and the fire his words had evoked inside him.

I need you. Without you we will fail. And that cannot happen. You are our last great hope and your deeds will be remembered for all time.

He tried to contain his excitement at the prospect of the upcoming mission. After today, Ibrahim would be able to serve his people in a way he'd never dreamed possible. Today's package would not be handed off to another. Today's package was for him. The instructions had been clear. His name would forever be etched into the stones of history. His people would sing his praise and the Americans would tremble in fear at the indomitable strength of The Seven.

The heat of the burning cigarette warmed his stained fingers as the embers closed in on the moist filter. Without wasting a moment, he retrieved another from the pack balanced on his thigh. He used the nearly spent cigarette to light his next, a true definition of a chain smoker. He flicked the butt out the small opening in the window, adding to the pile accumulating outside the door of his powder-blue Subaru Forester. He liked the "soccer mom" anonymity of this car.

It was hard for him to wait, but his instructions had been explicitly clear.

Wait a full hour. Ensure no counter-surveillance. Retrieve the package and proceed to the staging area.

The remaining minutes of that hour ticked by in timeless fashion. He scanned the area, looking for the exhaust of an idling vehicle. Ibrahim's Forester had been off for hours. He'd been prepared for the cool spring air, layering warm thermals under his jeans and sweatshirt. The only indication he was in the car was the smoke seeping out from his window, but he decided it was a minor risk at exposure. *How could he be expected to pass the time otherwise?* he had thought before lighting the first cigarette out of the now nearly empty pack.

Nothing on the street indicated he was being watched. The last car he'd seen had pulled onto the street twenty minutes ago and parked. The occupants, an elderly couple, shuffled into their multifamily brownstone without a look in his direction. The street was quiet, and the timing of the delivery had been purposeful. The carrier's instructions were clear. *Deliver between one and two p.m. Leave on doorstep.* Ibrahim had tracked the package using the postal app on his cell phone and was pleased when he watched the delivery truck pull down the street at 1:17 p.m. That was fifty-seven minutes ago.

Satisfied he was alone, Ibrahim stepped out of his vehicle, dropping the cigarette at his foot. He pulled the baseball cap brim low, obscuring his face from any potential video cameras in the area. Ibrahim moved purposefully down the uneven sidewalk in this quiet neighborhood located in the heart of Virginia's historic district of Old Towne Alexandria. His pace slowed as he neared the former residence of Debbie Johnson. Conducting one more visual scan of his surroundings, Ibrahim moved up the three weathered stone steps to the landing where the package rested.

The box was surprisingly light for the size of the box, but he knew the deadly contents contained therein and its devastating payload. He cradled the awkward shape of the box against his chest and returned the way he'd come. Keys in hand, he hit the trunk release and the back of the small-sized SUV's tailgate raised as he approached. He leaned forward, placed the box on the black carpeted lining of the trunk. He stood erect, stepped back, and closed the trunk, hearing the click of the latch.

Ibrahim's head was forced forward, striking the heavy tint of the trunk's window. His vision was peppered with speckles of light, like glitter flickering in the dark. The pain from the impact to his neck was crippling and his knees had buckled. He never felt the needle plunge into his neck. The glitter-filled haze faded to absolute darkness as one thought fluttered across Ibrahim's mind. *Failure.*

21

"Well that went smooth as bread pudding," Gator said.

"What about his car?" Nick asked.

"It will probably be tagged as a non-residentially parked vehicle or considered abandoned. Eventually it'll be towed and then sit in some lot indefinitely. No evidence of a crime. And no evidence of us being there."

Gator drove. The big man looked odd behind the wheel. Like he belonged in a gorilla cage and not wedged behind the dark finish of the Durango's dashboard. He struck a large pothole and the vehicle bounced violently. Nick's eyes widened.

Gator gave a hearty laugh. "Don't worry. I checked and it's not armed."

"That's a relief. How long's our friend back there going to be out of commission?" Nick asked.

"Probably an hour. Maybe a bit longer."

Nick nodded. "So, who funds our little group? I mean we had a Gulfstream on standby to shoot us across the country from Texas to the D.C. area. Private jets seem like a hefty budget item on an expense sheet," Nick said sarcastically.

"That's not really in my wheelhouse. Jay would be the one to ask if you're really interested. I find it better not to go looking that gift horse in the mouth, ya know?" Gator said in his thick accent. "I just know that we operate at a level well beyond any unit I've ever worked with. I like my new station in life and so I don't push too hard for answers I may not want the answer to." His last comment didn't carry the typical lightheartedness Nick had come to expect from the man.

"Understood." Nick looked back at the blanket covering the bound man sprawled across the seat and weighed his next question carefully, "So, how'd you end up here."

Gator let out a long sigh, "Well, you are the inquisitive type. I guess that makes sense. Jay and Declan said interviewing was your forte. I know the whole call sign thing seems a bit extreme, but it's done in part to provide an extra layer of protection."

"Protection?"

"If we end up like sleeping beauty back there. Stuffed into some bad guy's car and dragged off to who-knows-where to have who-knows-what done to us," Gator said.

Nick nodded, understanding the implication. "It just seems like you all know a hell of a lot about me and I just thought..."

"I'll say this. Jay found me when I was at a low point. Not too much different than you," Gator said.

"How so?"

"I was locked up too," Gator said, looking over at Nick. "Overseas. I did some wet work for an off-the-books CIA op. It got some bad press and I became the Army's patsy for the fallout. They labeled me a war criminal."

"Jesus," Nick muttered.

"Tell me about it. So, without boring you with details, I died. Like you." Gator cleared his throat. "And here I am. Just like you."

"Jay's op got you jammed up?" Nick asked.

Gator looked ahead. "He's loyal to those who are loyal to him. He told me you're cut from the same cloth in that regard."

Nick gave a half smile.

"He also said you're a hard man to kill. And to me those are two qualities that can't be taught," Gator said with a nod of approval.

"Thanks. Hopefully, I can live up to my reputation."

"Your buddy Declan—correction Ace—spoke highly of your abilities in regard to interrogation," Gator said.

"I guess. Seems like a lifetime ago now," Nick said dismissively.

"Well, you're about to see some next-level shit with Spider," Gator said.

"I understand everyone's nicknames except for his. Why Spider?" Nick asked.

"Because he traps people. The more you squirm and try to wiggle out of his interrogation, the more tangled you become, like a fly trapped in a spider's web." Gator laughed. "I wouldn't want him poking around in my head. That's for damn sure. Not too sure what the hell he'd find."

"I guess this guy's not going to have that luxury," Nick said, thumbing in the direction of their unconscious prisoner.

"The Spider is already spinning his web. And this little fly doesn't have any idea what's in store for him."

22

To say the room was dark didn't do justice to the word. The twelve square feet of space was void of any light. Even as Nick peered in through the thick glass of the one-way mirror, he couldn't make out the faintest outline of the man who was strapped to the chair inside. The only reason he knew the man was in the room was because he and Gator had been the ones who put him in there.

Nick thought of the box truck and his awakening into this strange new life. The man in that room was soon to wake from his sedative-induced slumber into the murky blackness surrounding him. How strange it would be to open your eyes and see nothing. The man would be blind to his unfamiliar circumstance. Then there was the silence to contend with.

Gator had referred to the room as The Cube and explained that their unit used rooms like this often and had them at various sites, or vaults as they called the office, which were staggered across the continental U.S. He had also shared the room's design. The walls were triple layered, basically a club sandwich of poured concrete and next-gen soundproofing. Gator said that they'd tested its effectiveness. A gunshot couldn't be heard once a person was sealed inside. The man strapped to the bolted chair could hear nothing and see nothing. Blind and deaf is terribly disorienting. The longer this man sat, the deeper he would sink into madness.

"How long has he been in?" Spider's smooth voice interrupted Nick's thoughts.

Nick looked down at his watch. "Two hours."

Spider looked down at the tablet in his hand. "He's been awake for ninety-three minutes."

"How do you know that?" Nick asked.

"The sensors built into the chair monitor his vitals among other things," Spider said as his stoic face broke into the slightest of smiles.

"I told you this guy goes next-level with this stuff," Gator chuckled, slapping his large hand in the center of Nick's back.

Nick nodded, catching his breath after the big man's jovial blow. He did not want to be on the bad side of Gator's fist if he ever wielded those giant meat paws in anger. It'd be like getting hit by an anvil.

Spider tapped the flat glass screen with his finger and the interior of The Cube burst into a bright light, penetrating through the heavy tints of the one-way mirror. Nick looked away, caught off guard by the sudden radiance.

Nick's eyes compensated for the light and he looked back into the room. The man strapped to the chair writhed in agony. Tears streamed down his face. The white light bathed his tan skin. Nick watched intently as the man shook violently, swinging his head back and forth obviously desperate to find a reprieve. The chair, bolted to the ground, did not budge. The man's eyes were tightly closed and his cheeks curled, desperate to create a barrier to the light. By the man's reaction, his eyelids were having little effect at stopping his torment.

Then another tap on the tablet from Spider's finger and the light was immediately replaced by darkness. Spider tapped on the screen again. This time nothing seemed to happen. Nick peered over at the screen, trying to see if he could figure this new phase.

"Sound." Spider said, coolly. "Very loud."

Nick heard nothing. He pressed his hand firmly against the wall of The Cube and felt no vibration. He stepped back, impressed at the design.

"Like I said. You can't hear a gunshot through those walls," Gator boomed.

"Any coffee left?" Spider asked.

"I think Wiz just made a fresh pot," Gator said.

Spider turned and walked toward the break room, carrying the tablet under his hand like a book. Nick followed.

The break room was clean and had a variety of different coffee makers. Nick eyed the assortment and watched as Spider went straight for the large percolator, nestled between a Keurig and an espresso machine.

"All this fancy crap, and this seven-year-old percolator makes a better cup than all of them," Spider said.

"I hate to admit, but I've been a Keurig convert," Nick jested. "Although I have to admit I've had to adjust my tastes for the past year."

"Try this and tell me I'm wrong."

Spider handed over a blue mug filled with the steaming dark liquid. Nick cradled it with both hands. He held up his cup briefly in a sort of mock cheers and then took a sip. He swallowed the hot aromatic beverage and nodded his agreement. "You win. That's a life-changing cup of coffee."

Spider poured his and then placed the cup on the granite countertop. He looked down at the screen and flicked open the application designed to control and monitor The Cube. After entering a code into the digital keypad, the Cube's control panel populated the glass. Spider's fingers nimbly navigated the icons, this time he tapped several different controls before putting the tablet on the counter. He turned his attention to the coffee.

"I've never seen anything like that used in an interrogation before," Nick said.

"Our paths aren't so different you know. But as with the way things are within this unit, pasts hold no real relevance to our present," Spider said. "Although, you will need to learn my trade."

"Why's that?"

"Because I may not always be around," Spider said solemnly.

"Planning on retiring anytime soon?" Nick said, trying to lighten the tone.

"This unit has an unusually high turnover rate," Spider said. "And *retirement* is one way of putting it."

"How long do you keep someone in The Cube before entering?" Nick asked, taking the cue that today's interrogation would serve as an orientation lesson.

Spider took a long deliberate sip from his mug. He eyed the tablet and then looked at Nick. His eyes were dark and complimented his olive skin, indicative of an Italian descent. An air of intensity shrouded him and only seemed to lessen when he would break the façade with his almost imperceptible grin.

"Depends. In this particular case we have a tight timeline. That bomb has a destination and this group is known for redundancy, ensuring a failsafe. Although, that was before we began to intervene. The numbers of The Seven have greatly dwindled in the last two years since you last had contact with them."

Nick watched the grin bend the edges of Spider's lips upward.

"Let's go spend a little time with our visitor and see how he's doing," Spider said, moving out of the kitchen area, tablet in one hand and coffee in the other. He strode to The Cube with the casualness of someone walking their dog.

Nick looked at the one-way mirror. Pulsating flashes of light shot out through the mirrored pane of glass. He approached and looked in at the man trapped inside. The strobe effect was intense, and the man flailed more wildly than before. His face had tuned a bright red in anguish and his mouth opened and closed. Nick could tell the man was screaming, although no sound penetrated The Cube.

"Heavy metal music is now accompanying the light show," Spider said, matter-of-factly.

Then the room went dark again. Within thirty seconds the strobe started again.

"He may not be ready yet, but time isn't on our side. I'd normally continue this for another couple hours before making contact. But we do what we can with the cards we're dealt," Spider said, turning off the lights and sound with a quick barrage of finger strokes of his tablet. The overhead light came on and the room now looked like an ordinary interview room. A table separated the restrained man from the other chair in the room. Spider pressed his index finger on a panel next to the door. There was a beep and then a hiss as the seal released. The door slid silently along the track. It reminded Nick of the cell he'd called home for the past year. *But as Spider said—our pasts no longer matter.*

Nick watched from behind the one-way glass as the door's mechanics shut the door behind Spider, entering the room to face off with the restrained man.

"You son of bitch!" Ibrahim screamed. His voice squeaked. The rasp was a combination of his lifetime of smoking which was further exacerbated by his recent bellowing.

Spider ignored the man and sat, adjusting himself into the soft cushioned chair and pulling himself neatly to the table. He set the tablet on the table and looked at the man seated before him.

Ibrahim was wet with perspiration. His tan skin was blotched darker from the physical exertion in his futile resistance to the light and sound immersion he'd received. His breathing came in ragged spurts. He looked down at the floor, away from Spider's intense eyes.

"We are going to talk about some things. Most of which you do not want to talk about," Spider said, speaking slowly and calmly. "Do you understand this?"

"I'm not saying anything! You can go to hell!" Ibrahim spat the words.

Spider cocked his head to the side, evaluating the unsuspecting fly trapped in his net. His face held no trace of emotion. He allowed a moment of silent reflection to pass before speaking again.

"That would be a shame. If you're not ready to talk, then I'll have to leave. If I leave then it starts again," Spider said whirling his index finger in the air. He could see the restrained man's understanding register in his face.

Ibrahim opened his mouth to say something and then closed it. He sighed deeply and the heave of his chest showed his resignation.

Spider had read the intelligence report gathered by Wiz and knew that Ibrahim was psychologically weak. He knew it would take very little to overwhelm the man's will to fight, especially after the last couple of hours he'd spent inside The Cube.

The room could challenge the strongest of minds. Spider knew this because he'd managed to spend seventy-two hours in there before teetering on the brink of insanity. The other members told him he was foolish to do it, but he had explained that to understand a weapon's potency you must experience it first-hand. It was a lesson he'd learned from his hapkido instructor. *You can't effectively deliver a strike until you've felt its impact.*

"Would you like me to leave?" Spider asked, the veiled threat was obvious.

Ibrahim said nothing but raised his head slightly, sheepishly making eye contact.

"Good. Now, with that out of the way, we can begin our conversation," Spider said. "I need you to understand how things work inside here. Once you fully comprehend the capabilities of this room and how it can be used, we can begin a meaningful dialog."

Ibrahim's eyes fluttered as he quickly scanned the bare walls of the room before settling back on Spider.

"The chair you're strapped to is very special and relatively unique in its design. It's reading your vitals, body temperature, weight distribution, and muscle tension as you sit there. I tell you this, so you understand the importance of truthfulness. I'm very good at detecting deception without any of this, but I like to remove all doubt. You'll find that I am very thorough in my job. Your body will tell me when you're being honest and when you're not. I need you to understand this because your honesty is the only thing keeping you from returning to the dark."

Spider tapped the screen on the tablet and looked at the display. He examined the sensory input, watching as the man's breathing rate increased along with his heart rate. A lot of physiological reactions were taking place inside Ibrahim's body. Spider was satisfied the previous two hours had the desired effect.

"I can see you don't want the darkness again," Spider said softly.

"What do you want from me? Who are you?" Ibrahim hissed.

"We'll get to that. Or maybe not. Your questions are irrelevant. I will ask and you will answer truthfully. Do you understand what I told you? About this room, your chair, and the importance of telling the truth?"

"Yes."

"If we get to an impasse and you're unwilling to be truthful then I'll have to step out. You don't want me to do that," Spider said. "Resistance is wasted energy."

"Whatever you think you can do to me, they can do worse," Ibrahim said flatly.

"Let's start there. Who is *they*?"

Ibrahim hesitated, breaking eye contact.

"Well, we're not getting off to a good start. I can see you don't understand the position you're in. I'll give you some time to think," Spider said, pushing his chair back.

Ibrahim's eyes immediately widened, panic stricken at the sudden movement of his interrogator. "Wait. Please don't leave me in here. I just need a minute. Please! They'll kill me! You know that? If you've done your research, then you know how dangerous they are."

"Weren't you just about to blow yourself up? And you sit there worried about death. I thought they picked you because of your resolve. Sounds to me like they picked the wrong man for the job," Spider said, casting an eye of judgment.

"I'm prepared to die!" Ibrahim yelled.

Spider tapped the screen, ignoring the man's outburst. He looked at the vitals and smiled. "No, you're not. You're terrified. Of me. Of them. You're definitely no martyr. They must be really desperate to pick you for such a task."

"They picked me. They know who Ibrahim Al Faziq is and what I'm capable of!" His hands dug into the armrests, nearly peeling back his fingernails.

"Who is *they*?" Spider asked again. "Let's assume I know, and this is my first test of your truthfulness. Lies have consequences."

"The Seven!" Ibrahim said through gritted teeth. A froth of spit bubbled out, coating his lower lip in the white substance.

"Now that wasn't so hard was it? I hope everything I ask you isn't going to be this difficult. It'll be a very long conversation if you decide to behave this way. You need to get past the fact that you've failed. To be honest, we probably saved you from botching your mission. Consider yourself lucky," Spider said.

"Lucky?" Ibrahim asked.

"From what I see there was a good chance you would've screwed up and then they'd probably take out your failure by punishing your son. Can you imagine what they'd do to him?"

"My son? How do you know about my son?" Ibrahim asked, his face contorting into a pained expression.

"We know everything about you."

"If you touch my son, I'll—"

"You'll do nothing. Understand that. Get that through your head and know that your threats are wasted on me and the people I work with. Your son is fine for now, but how long I'm able to guarantee his safety will depend on your cooperation," Spider said, emotionless.

Ibrahim sat speechless.

Spider tapped an icon on the tablet. The Cube's speaker system came to life.

"Father? Is that you? Father? Where are you? It's so dark in here. Help me please!" Spider ended the transmission and looked up at the restrained man.

Ibrahim's last reserve of resistance leaked out of him in the form of tears streaming down the deflated expression on his face. "Please—he's my only son. He's only a boy. Only fifteen. Don't hurt him."

"He's in a room just like this. Waiting. Just like you waited. It's dark in there," Spider said evenly. "How long can a child's mind handle the dark before falling apart?"

"You're sick! He's just a boy!"

"What were you going to blow up? Children and families would've been killed. I don't want to hurt your son, but like I said that depends on you."

"Anything. Just don't hurt him. I'll tell you anything you want," Ibrahim said, his shoulders went slack, and his head slumped in defeat.

* * *

"Pretty cool stuff, huh?" Wiz said.

Wiz's comment startled Nick who was fully engrossed in the audio feed from the interrogation. Nick was sitting at his cubicle. He wore headphones and had been listening to Spider's interrogation. Although the room was silent, there was a microphone and video recording device in place, allowing others in the unit to monitor.

"We've got his kid in one of these Cube things? What the hell is going on here? I'm all for saving lives, but torturing kids?" Nick said angrily.

"Relax. It's fabricated. His son's at home with his mother. I was able to reconstruct the message from conversations we'd intercepted. Pretty damn effective though?" Wiz asked.

"Very," Nick said, settling his nerves.

"I told you. The Spider's got skills," Gator boomed as he walked by with a large burrito in hand.

"I guess I got some things to learn," Nick said, slipping the headset back on to listen to the interrogation.

24

"At least it wasn't on the other side of the country. I hate flying and avoid it at all costs. But sometimes these ops don't afford me that luxury," Gator said, his bulk conforming to the confines of the SUV driver's seat.

Nick looked over at the large man and chuckled to himself at the sight. He couldn't imagine the man's muscular girth would fit comfortably in any vehicle. They should have towed him on a flatbed.

The prep for this op had been very detailed, especially considering the limited time frame before its execution. Jay was initially convinced the snatch of Ibrahim would've adjusted the timeline and bought them some time. Then Wiz intercepted some chatter and confirmed Spider's assumption that The Seven didn't have much faith in Ibrahim's ability to complete the task. When Ibrahim hadn't responded to them, they'd assumed he'd chickened out. A second man had been tasked with carrying out the attack. Redundancy was critical to any mission success and The Seven were desperately looking for a win.

Gator and Nick sat in the postal delivery truck in the back lot of the Post Office on Cameron Street. The windows were heavily tinted, blocking any view in through the windows. The bottle-nosed front end faced a four-foot concrete privacy wall separating the rear of the postal parking lot from another strip of businesses.

The red-bricked sidewalks were quiet, as they should be on a Sunday morning in Alexandria's historic Old Towne. All of the neighboring businesses were closed at the moment and most would remain so for the day. Only one building had activity from its arriving patrons.

The Christ Church, built at the conclusion of the Revolutionary War, had stood the test of time. It was the church attended by sitting presidents until the turn of the 21st Century. It was, however, chosen by The Seven for a different reason. During World War II, Roosevelt and Churchill had attended the church in a ceremony to commemorate the World Day of Prayer for Peace. The Seven, in the manifesto set for release and intercepted by Wiz, sought to taint this landmark and make it a call to war.

The team had arrived a few hours earlier under the cover of darkness. A microdrone had done overflight surveillance before they entered the area. The same drone now acted as their overwatch. Cameron Street was the side of the church where Ibrahim had been directed to stage his phase of the attack. That intel was the reason Nick and the large man from the Bayou were manning their current post.

Gator and Nick were positioned at a good vantage point to the street and church. Declan and Barbie had just walked into the building to attend the church service. They were tasked with scouting a secondary assault team.

Spider extracted an incredible amount of detail from their captive. The plan called for an external detonation in the form of a car bomb, a task originally meant for Ibrahim that now was assigned to his replacement. The force of the blast was designed to crumple several of the load-bearing walls of the historic structure, collapsing the church's pulpit and forcing panicked parishioners toward the front doors. Two additional martyrs would be inside and tasked with detonating a secondary device as the people exited, effectively turning the ornate church into a fiery tomb.

The Seven's plan was complicated. It called for simultaneous actions by each team operating without any on-site communication. A vehicle, the replacement to Ibrahim's powder blue Subaru, would pull up and activate its hazards. The driver had been instructed to give the appearance of being broken down or out of gas. He'd idle in the lane closest to the church on Cameron's one-way street. The man in the car would be instructed to wait for five minutes after the church doors closed and then detonate. Those were the instructions Ibrahim had been given and the team had to assume would still be in place.

Nick and Gator had to close the gap and take out that threat without allowing him the opportunity to activate the detonator. Declan and Barbie had the tougher job of eliminating the interior threat in a crowd full of civilians. Wiz controlled the drone from his cubicle and would use it to jam any potential remote detonation capabilities while Gator disabled the car bomb.

25

Declan moved into the church's interior. The air was thick with a damp mustiness coated by the overwhelming fragrant incense. The combination of conflicting odors was comparable to someone masking body odor with perfume.

Barbie held his hand, giving the illusion the two were a happy couple. The cool early morning air allowed for both to wear long overcoats. The ensemble enabled them to effectively conceal the weapons strapped to their waists without drawing any unusual glances from the other patrons. Declan took two long, controlled breaths as they slowly approached a row of pews near the back of the church.

Hands held, they both scanned the crowd. A man of middle eastern descent stood near the back wall, alone. His eyes were closed, and he appeared to be praying. Declan assumed he actually might be, but figured his prayer was more for strength rather than salvation. Either way he was definitely one of The Seven's two inside men. He too, wore a jacket and the bulk of it was most likely due to the explosive rig strapped to his chest. Declan gave a squeeze of Barbie's hand and then traced his pinkie finger across her palm, indicating the direction of the man he'd targeted. She shot a glance at the man and then squeezed his hand twice indicating she understood.

Barbie located the second man. He was in a pew two rows up from them. This man also wore a puffy winter coat.

"Hey hon, I'm just going to hit the restroom," Declan said, releasing Barbie's hand.

Barbie nodded and Declan slid past her, exiting to the center aisle. He moved purposefully, proceeding to the rear of the church without looking at the man in the back, who would be Declan's target. He entered the restroom and locked the door.

Declan withdrew the pistol from his waist. It had a longer draw because of the silencer threaded to the barrel. He'd decided it was a better idea for him to prep this weapon into position while out of the public's view.

Barbie's large handbag was empty except for one item. At the bottom rested a pistol, also affixed with a silencer. The purse enabled easier access at the point in time when she'd need to retrieve it.

The silencers would minimize any initial shock wave of panic from the civilians present. After the assault, crowd control and their subsequent escape would be the next biggest hurdle in this operation.

26

"A small minivan just rolled to a stop on Cameron. Hazards on. Target acquired. We're moving," Nick said. His voice was clear, and all of the other members of the team would receive the message through the flesh-colored wireless earbud inserted in his left ear.

In the short time he'd been involved in this unit, the technology available amazed Declan. That was no small feat, impressing someone who'd been hand-plucked from the Navy's elite SEAL teams for selection in the ghost unit, Alpha One. The earbud was actually more like a Band-Aid, an eighth of an inch in diameter adhered to the skin. To see it, someone would've had to be standing next to him and staring into his earlobe. The sound quality was unrivaled in anything he'd used in the past. Nick's last transmission sounded as though he was standing beside him. Wiz told him it had another unique capability in its proprietary design. The earpiece would adjust volume to outside influences like gunfire or explosions, enabling them to hear clearly under the worst of combat conditions. Or as Jay had put it, *if the shit hit the proverbial fan.*

The processional hymn began. Declan exited the restroom and watched as the priest ambled slowly behind a young altar boy swinging the decorative incense ball against the chain. The smell intensified, adding to the lingering remnants he'd smelled earlier.

Declan had his hands inside his coat pockets. In his right he held the silenced 9mm. He had cut out the interior seam of the jacket's pocket, enabling him to maintain a solid grip on the gun without exposing any of it.

He stopped short before crossing from the hallway into the interior of the church and into view of the target. The heavy wood of the church's front doors banged loudly as they closed. The Seven timeline had begun. Five minutes until the car bomb was set to go off.

"Can I help you find your seat sir?" A well-dressed usher asked.

"No thanks. I think I'll stand close to the restroom. I've got a bit of a stomach bug. A little Montezuma's Revenge," Declan said.

The last comment had the desired effect. At hearing about his sickness, the man moved away from Declan and stepped deeper into the church and off to the right. This gave Declan an unobstructed entrance point when the time came.

27

For a big man, Gator moved like a cat, nimbly closing the gap between their postal truck to the idling minivan. Nick intentionally lagged behind as they'd planned during their rehearsal preparations. Gator wore a postal delivery uniform and approached the man in the vehicle, walking around the rear of the minivan to the driver's side. They'd banked on the fact that the man in the vehicle would be too nervous to notice the uniform as being out of place for a Sunday.

Gator tapped on the glass of the driver's side window. "Hey there, fella! Can I give you a hand?" Gator asked in his thick Louisiana accent.

The man almost jumped at the interruption. Seeing the uniform, he softened slightly and shook his head. Sweat poured from the man's forehead. Although tan in complexion, he looked pale and was obviously overcome by his unnerving task. Blowing one's self up was no simple undertaking.

Gator laughed loudly. "Really friend, it's no trouble whatsoever. Pop the hood and I'll take a look for ya."

The man in the car shook his head again, and the fear originally lining his face now shifted to anger.

Gator stood by the window drawing the man's attention as Nick deftly moved to the front of the minivan.

Nick raised the pistol in his hand and took aim at the man's forehead. The man turned and Nick fired three times. The silencer muted most of the sound. Most of the noise came from the 9mm rounds as they penetrated the windshield. The glass had one hole with cracks spiderwebbing out from its center. The second and third rounds had followed the path of the first one, a testament to Nick's precision.

The man's head had rocked back at the initial impact but came to rest in a slumped forward manner. The headshots had served their intended purpose, bringing death to the bomber and immediately interrupting the brain's function as to prevent the man from detonating the device in hand.

"Target one down. Working on disabling the package," Gator said through the bone mic taped to his throat.

"Two minutes," Jay's voice transmitted. "Ace and Barbie are up."

* * *

Declan heard the transmission and eyed the back of his partner's head, waiting for her cue. The trick of killing two men at the same time was a skill few were capable of. More challenging was to do it surrounded by hundreds of unaware civilians. Both Declan and Barbie had Homeland Security badges affixed to their hips and had rehearsed their follow-up. But the execution of such dynamic plans always carried inherent, and often unforeseen, variables.

The congregation stood as the priest greeted the crowd. Barbie stood with them. Declan watched her intently as she began deliberately moving her head up and down as if answering a question. Once, twice, and on the third bob of her head Barbie's right arm swung up quickly. The purse dropped to the wooden bench seat as her arm extended with the silenced pistol in hand.

Declan stepped out from around the corner and into the church, planting and pivoting his foot while taking up a stable shooting platform. His gun's front sight came up on the target as he moved. Two shots exited his weapon as his marked man turned his attention to Barbie as she fired on the other target.

The shots found their mark and both men collapsed. The man Barbie had shot fell forward and was bent over the hardwood backing of the pew in front of him. Her target had been more difficult than Declan's. In the split second allotted, she had to ensure the angle of shot would have a safe backdrop.

As predicted, shrieks erupted at the sight of the two dead men. Several parishioners nearest Barbie's target had been painted in the man's blood, adding to the fervor of the screams.

Declan and Barbie shouted at the crowd, "Homeland Security! Calmly exit the main doors of the church! Do it now!" As they gave their rehearsed commands both of them exposed the badges on their hips.

Declan and Barbie quickly moved to their respective targets. The rigging of the bomb vests each martyr wore were identical and simple in design. At the sight of the bombs, a new wave of panicked cries rippled through the crowd. They separated the detonators from each brick of C4, rendering the bombs safe. The church cleared out into the street and quiet was restored to its interior.

Declan and Barbie made for the exit nearest the pulpit, and furthest away from the recently departed crowd. They reversed their jackets and donned knit caps as they stepped from the church. The quick change gave them a modicum of disguise as they worked their way to their postal van.

Gator drove out of the area as Wiz guided them by drone,

avoiding the responding police cruisers. Nick let his hair out of the tight ponytail, and it fell wildly about his face and shoulders.

"Jesus buddy, your name really fits," Declan said.

"How's that?" Nick asked.

"You really look like a wolf."

The group laughed, releasing the tension of the morning's mission. Nick's first official indoctrination had been completed. He replayed the event in his mind as the church disappeared into the background.

28

Back at the office everyone went about their business with the same casualness as if they'd just returned from getting coffee. Nick was still adjusting to this new life and sat quietly at the conference table. It had been a long time since he'd fired a weapon and taken a life. It was a burden he never took lightly, no matter the target.

"You good?" Declan asked, pulling up a seat and plopping heavily into it.

"Yeah. Just taking a minute to let this whole cloak and dagger thing sink in," Nick said. "Not really my forte."

Declan shed his typical cavalier demeanor and dropped his cocky smile. Straight-faced he said, "You did good today. Lots of innocents would've died if you hadn't taken that shot."

"I know," Nick said. "Thanks."

Declan looked down at his watch. "I've got to run. Val's been without me for a while. I'm heading home for a bit. I've got to make the six-hour drive up to Connecticut. Hoping to make it there by dinner. I'll be back in a few days or when the next mission spins up. Need anything?" Declan asked.

"Nope. Say hi to Val and the girls for me."

"I can't."

"Huh?"

"You're dead, remember?" Declan's smile returned. "Unless I told them I've been hanging out with your ghost. Not sure how that'd go over."

Nick feigned a smile as Declan departed.

"Speaking of the dead. Since our last operation left no one alive to interrogate, I guess that frees us up a bit," Jay said, obviously having heard Declan's comment when exiting his office and entering the main space. "How'd you like to go to a funeral?"

"Whose?" Nick asked.

"Yours."

29

"Tobie we're late! Let's go!" Kemper yelled up the stairs.

The sound of gunfire and explosions erupted from the second floor.

"Tobie Daniel Jones get down here this instant! Now!" Kemper Jones boomed.

The effort caused his face to redden. He hoped he didn't have to stomp up the stairs in the uncomfortable suit he was wearing. He hadn't had many occasions in recent years requiring this level of dress. His daily attire was usually a button-down collared shirt and a pair of 5.11 Tactical khakis with some flex built into the waist.

The last time he'd adorned the charcoal suit's coat and pants was when he had been promoted to detective several years back. Its fit had been tight. Now, it almost cut off the circulation to his legs. A valiant attempt to button his pants had left him winded and extremely frustrated. He'd finally given up, resolving to leave it unbuttoned. His belt was the only thing keeping the trousers up. He fumed and decided he'd be damned before he would climb those stairs to get his son, fearful the effort might render him pantless.

"Coming!" Tobie shouted over the volume of his video game.

"Now!" Kemper shouted in response.

Tobie looked at the words on the screen in front of him. He was elated. A few friends at school had achieved this and he'd been trying ever since.

The message read: *Congratulations PROSPECT!*

He noticed a new message alert from a player whose gamer handle was Graham_CrackerHacker. Tobie could hear his father losing his patience and fearing another blow out, logged off. His dad had been on edge ever since Agent Lawrence had been locked up, and the news of his death had a devastating effect. He worried about his dad, but wasn't sure how to help. During his rotational stays at his dad's apartment he'd been spending more time immersed with his online gaming than any real quality time with his old man. He regretted the decline of their relationship and hoped they'd find a way to reconnect.

Throwing on his navy-blue blazer coat, Tobie Jones bounded down the stairs two at a time.

"Son, I swear on everything good and holy, you're going to be late to your own funeral," Kemper said, trying to calm his frustration. There had been some recent tension between the two and Kemper knew most of it stemmed from his ex-wife's recently remarrying. His son was a good kid but he could tell the change in lifestyle was having an impact.

Tobie rolled his eyes and brushed past his father. "Come on dad, we don't want to be late."

Sarcasm, a teenager's ultimate weapon, and as of late Tobie deployed it on his father with increased regularity. Kemper shook his head, shaking off the jibe as he huffed after his son into the unseasonably warm air. March in Texas was a strange transitional period and provided a short, almost imperceptible, shift from winter into summer.

30

"Wiz already has it cued up," Jay said, waving his arm in the direction of the tech genius hunched over his keyboard.

Nick said nothing. He stood and followed Jay over to where Wiz was seated.

"I took the liberty of launching a drone from our facility outside of Austin," Wiz said, looking up from the array of screens before him.

"Austin?" Nick asked.

"Anaya received a death notification from the prison. At the initial phases of your incarceration, you'd listed her as your only next of kin to be notified in the event of your death."

"Jesus, I totally forgot about that." Nick's stomach sank at the thought of delivering another blow to the woman he'd loved and had planned on starting a life with. His past cost them their baby. And now his death, although staged, would pick at the emotional scab.

"She arranged to have you buried in a cemetery close by to her home," Jay said.

Nick sighed.

"Everyone always wonders what their funeral would look like.

Funny thing about death is nobody ever gets to find out. But you get a sneak peek, watching it first hand," Wiz said with a geeky smile.

Nick leaned in, looking at the empty grave and the mound of freshly upturned dirt piled beside it. The casket hovered above the hole, cradled by two thick straps wrapped around the rolling cylinders running parallel to the length of the brown wood of the box. A caretaker in dirt-covered gray overalls stood off to the side and out of the way standing under the shade of a tree. Near the foot of the casket stood a heavyset middle-aged man in a cheaply made suit. Nick did not recognize either man—obviously they were employed by the funeral home or cemetery. The 4K image fed from the drone hovering silently above was as clear as if Nick had been perched in a nearby tree.

"How about we give him a minute alone?" Jay asked, nudging Wiz.

Wiz looked at Jay and then over to Nick. He nodded and stood, vacating his seat. Wiz gestured for Nick to take his spot in front of the monitors. "Try not to touch anything. I get the feeling you're not the most tech-savvy of people. The drone's autopilot is set and will remain in its current position, automatically adjusting for winds and other environmental variances."

Nick said nothing as he slipped into Wiz's chair, adjusting himself.

It was strange, almost surreal to look out on his burial site. Nick was aware the ceremony was a ruse to further mask his disappearance from his former life. He looked at the solitude in which his body was to be buried. Minus a few, those closest to him were dead. An empty funeral spoke volumes to the life he had lead, or at least to the choices he'd made.

Anaya Patel entered the drone's field of vision. She wore a dark dress. Her long black hair shimmered in the sunlight and her mocha brown skin contrasted with the bright white of the flowers she cradled in the crux of her arm.

The sight of her had a crippling effect. A rush of emotion flooded him, feelings and thoughts he had tucked deep during his year's incarceration came to the forefront. Nick leaned closer to the monitor.

Kemper Jones appeared in view, trotting across the rough St. Augustine grass. Nick watched as his portly friend's hustle was impeded by his tight-fitting suit. The Austin detective's bulk bulged out at various spots. Knowing the man as well as Nick did after working several cases of depravity together, he was aware of his disdain for such dress. Nick appreciated his friend's effort but couldn't help chuckle at his appearance. Kemper Jones' teenage son followed in step behind him.

Nick watched as Kemper gave Anaya a long, heart-felt embrace. He longed to feel her skin against his and smell its sweet familiarity. The thought was a fleeting one and he sadly knew the reality, that he would never hold her again.

Anaya and Kemper separated, and they looked in the direction of the casket. A moment passed where time seemed to stand still for Nick. Had it not been for the fluttering branches of a nearby tree, he would have thought the screen image was frozen.

Anaya nodded to the man in the suit who, in turn, nodded to the caretaker under the tree. And with that Nick Lawrence's funeral service, or lack thereof, came to its close.

The caretaker pulled the lowering wench and the casket began its controlled descent into the ground. The three attendees looked on with heads bowed. Anaya broke from her solace and took a step toward the hole, tossing in the flowers.

Nick looked more closely and noticed she had something else in her left hand, something he hadn't seen until now. It looked like a small stuffed animal. Anaya pressed the plush blue bear to her lips and threw it atop the brown wood of the casket. She gently caressed her stomach, touching the emptiness.

"Wiz, can you zoom this thing?" Nick called over his shoulder.

Wiz appeared and tapped a few keys on one of the nearby keyboards. He then grabbed a controller. "What do you want to see?"

"The stuffed animal on top of the casket," Nick said, straining his eyes hoping to get a better look.

Wiz manipulated the controller, and the image enlarged without losing any of the clarity. The camera zoomed in to such a degree Nick was able to read the tag attached to the bear's collar. *Nick Jr.*

Nick had shut out everyone in his life after his arrest. In doing so, he'd never learned whether the baby they'd lost was a boy or girl. At the time he deemed it one additional layer of emotional protection, a way to dissociate and distance himself. The newfound shock of this revelation rocked him to his core. He'd lost his son, a boy they'd never had an opportunity to name. Cut down before he had a chance at life, a twisted consequence to his actions several years before.

Nick closed his eyes but not before a tear found its exit. The salty discharge trickled down his face, becoming lost in the tangles of his unkempt beard.

"Sorry man. We just figured it would give you some closure," Wiz said softly.

Nick allowed the sadness to pass and opened his eyes. With one swift move of his arm, he removed any trace of the tear. Wiz had typed in some commands and the drone's live feed was now offline. A still image remained on the screen. Anaya's face, wet with tears, frozen in front of him. As painful as it was to see, a small part of him felt relieved she still cared for him and, maybe, still loved him. The way things ended had been tragic, and he never thought he would see her again. He was grateful for the opportunity, even if it was under these extremely unusual circumstances.

Jay clasped Nick's shoulder, the same shoulder he'd taken three bullets in when saving the former CIA operative's life. "I think you could use a drink?"

"I can't think of anything better," Nick said.

The dim light added a nostalgic element to the Irish pub. The low rumble of conversation and laughter blended with the instrumental music piping through the speakers overhead. Nick followed Jay to a table against the wall.

"How many years has it been since we've sat in this bar?" Jay asked.

"Too many," Nick said. "A lot's changed since those days."

"No truer statement." Jay stopped talking as a waitress approached. He ordered two Black and Tans. As she walked away, he continued, "I know this is a lot to take in, but I think you're going to find that this is a good fit for you."

"How long have you been running this team?" Nick asked.

"I switched over about five years ago. There was a need for what we do. The country needed the ability to react quickly and decisively against rapidly evolving threats. I was picked to assemble the team. And the unit has evolved over the years through personnel and operational reach."

"Who do we work for?" Nick asked quietly.

Jay didn't answer. The waitress returned, placing the beers in front of the two before disappearing into the small crowd.

"That's a hard question to answer. Simplest answer, we're sanctioned at the highest levels. At the same time, we don't exist and therefore are expendable. If something breaks bad or one of us is killed, then we are on our own," Jay said. He then paused, taking a long pull from the mug. The dark of the Guinness swirled against the amber lager of the Harp as he set the glass down.

"I guess that makes sense. If it breaks wrong, then there would be no ties. Nobody to take the blame, but us," Nick said.

"Something like that," Jay said. He hesitated momentarily and then continued, "I couldn't watch you disappear into the abyss of that prison. I owed you."

Nick let the beer roll down his throat. "Speaking of my exodus from Masterson. Those three bodies used to replace Gator, Spider, and me."

"Not what you think. We didn't go off and kill a few people for the ruse. Jesus Nick, give me some credit," Jay said with a shake of his head.

"Well then how's it work?" Nick asked.

"We've got connections and are able to get bodies when needed. Most come from people who've donated their body to science. We are able to enter a variety of databases and have the manifests changed. The hardest part was finding close physical matches. You and Gator are atypical body types."

"Okay, but how did you pull off the medical transport? Wouldn't the jail realize the ambulance was phony when none of the neighboring hospitals or ambulance companies had been dispatched to Masterson?" Nick asked, rubbing his temples in a concerted effort to understand.

"Yes, but we mitigated by creating confusion. When you were a teenager did you ever tell one of your parents you were going to a friend's house? And the friend would say they were going to your house, but in reality you were going to a party somewhere else?" Jay asked.

"Yeah, but I don't get how that analogy applies to this," Nick said.

"We've basically done the same thing. Wiz manipulated the incoming and outgoing information from all of the involved departments. The medic employee files for Gator and Spider were embedded into an actual ambulance company. Long story short, three people died when the front right tire blew, and the ambulance struck a tree. We staged a fire which made the bodies unrecognizable," Jay said, smiling and obviously content with his summation.

"You went through all that trouble for me," Nick said, shaking his head.

"You know I would've been dead in the deserts of Afghanistan if it hadn't been for you. I don't take the debt of that day lightly," Jay said.

"I think we can call the debt paid."

"A life debt never feels fully repaid," Jay said sincerely. He cleared his throat and said, "I'm sorry about the funeral thing. I just thought it might give you some closure."

Nick nodded slightly. "I never really said goodbye. Thank you for giving me that. Crazy you're able to get a drone up and control it remotely. That's some military-level stuff."

"You have no idea what you are walking into with this unit."

"I'll adjust. I guess I don't have much choice," Nick said, running his condensation-covered hand through his long hair. "So, what's next?"

"Most of our operations come from assignments handed down from my boss. We also gather our own intel on prospective targets. Wiz scours databases looking for patterned criminalized behavior with large scale threat implications. If we come across something that might meet our operational capabilities, then I forward it up. Nothing we do happens without a green light. That means your extraction was sanctioned."

"Did you say boss?" Nick asked. "I thought we didn't answer to anyone?"

"Everyone is accountable to someone. Don't waste your energy on that equation," Jay said with a half-smile.

"What if I want out? What then?" Nick asked softly, looking down at the drink in his hand.

"You're a free man. You give me the word and you'll walk away. New identification and new life."

"With your boss's approval," Nick added.

Jay said nothing.

"Declan has a family. How long do you think he can operate like this?" Nick asked.

"He's a hell of an asset."

"That's not an answer," Nick said, draining the remains of his pint in one gulp.

"I guess that decision lies with him then," Jay said.

"He's only doing this because of me. I know he feels like he owes me too."

"Maybe. Probably. I don't know," Jay said. "I know one thing—he definitely believes in what we're doing. He sees the futility and bureaucracy when it comes to hunting the real threats. We cut the red tape. We can move at speeds beyond any other domestic agency's capabilities."

"I know. I got a taste of that this morning," Nick said. "It's just a bit beyond my norm. I'm an investigator, not an assassin."

"Were."

"Huh?"

"You *were* an investigator," Jay said. "Nick Lawrence, FBI agent, is dead."

Nick said nothing but intently looked into his friend's eyes. He'd found a way to adjust to life as an inmate and knew time would help him with this latest transition.

Jay flagged the waitress's attention and held up two fingers. Moments later two more black and tans appeared. The two men tapped the glasses together.

"Happy funeral day," Jay jested.

Nick laughed, "To many more."

32

The news stations had continued to air their coverage of Sheldon Price's school attack. Interviews of survivors trickled in as victims sought their fifteen minutes of fame. One particular boy's recounting of the events had caught the attention of Tanner Morris as he sat in the ornate conference room. The boy's name, Blake Johnson, was plastered on the digital banner beneath his face.

"There was all this shooting and explosions and stuff. Crazy—just crazy. I'm lucky to be alive," Blake Johnson said, looking distraught.

"You mentioned to me off-camera about something the shooter yelled before his rampage began. Can you share with our viewers what Sheldon Price screamed before opening fire on you and your classmates? Do you remember what he said?" The news anchor asked in rapid fire succession.

"Sasquatch 187," Tanner said.

"Sasquatch 187? Do you have any idea what that means?" the reporter asked.

"Nope. But I'll tell you this. Sheldon was a loner and a weirdo.

I just wished I had been able to stop him," Blake said with false bravado.

"You're a very brave young man! And you should be proud of yourself," the reporter said.

Tanner Morris hit mute and then turned, facing the members of his small council. "The test runs are complete. It's time to launch the final phase of our operation. Graham tells me he's secured Patriot level candidates in all fifty states."

The room was silent. The truth behind that statement carried a gravity and each member knew it. The only one who appeared genuinely pleased was Graham Morris.

"It's time to send the manifesto. It's time to wake this country from its slumber and open their eyes," Tanner said.

"The broadcast is ready," Graham said.

Simon Belfort, the technical genius who worked behind the scenes, chimed in, "It's anonymized and will be untraceable. Well, I'm sure they'll eventually track it down, but I've set it up so that even when they do it will never lead back to us."

"Very well. Send it," Tanner said.

Belfort nodded and left the room. He returned a few moments later. "It's done."

Graham Morris smiled broadly and had a glint of madness in his eyes. It was a look Tanner had seen in his son many times in the past. The blood lust of his only heir worried him, but he pushed the thought from his mind and turned his attention back to the television mounted on the wall.

Tanner Morris turned up the volume on the newscast and sank into the worn leather of his chair, waiting for the media to deliver his message.

33

"We've got a problem," Wiz said aloud to all present.

"What's up?" Jay asked.

"Check it out for yourself. It's breaking on all the stations right now," Wiz said, looking up from his computer and clicking on the television.

At the top of the screen a bright red banner with the bold-faced words BREAKING NEWS came into view. A panic-stricken blonde reporter in a light-blue power suit looked wide-eyed as she shuffled papers and cleared her throat.

"This station has just received a disturbing message. We are still in the process of confirming its authenticity, but we wanted to bring it to you immediately. Remember, you heard it here first!"

Barbie smirked, "Why does the blonde always have to be the dipshit?" For affect, she flipped her strawberry blonde hair in an exaggerated arc like an actress on a shampoo commercial.

"Not all. Just this one," Gator said in his thick accent.

"Shh. You'll want to hear this," Wiz said.

"The message you're about to hear is a disturbing one and this station recommends that if young children are present please have them leave the room at this time." The reporter waited for approximately ten seconds, adding to the dramatic effect of her delivery. "We'll play it for you now."

A mechanical voice replaced the refined reporter's delivery:

"This message is to those who have preyed on the weak, picking on and isolating those classmates who you deemed unworthy of your friendship. A reckoning is coming.

This battle has been long fought but has remained invisible to many and condoned by societal silence. Every day children are victimized by the brutal attacks of their peers. These attacks, both physically and emotionally, have demoralized and irreversibly damaged innocent children.

Our schools have become breeding grounds for bullies. Our educational system has turned a blind eye to these travesties. Governmental attempts to address this through catchy slogans and feel-good initiatives have failed. Teenage suicide is on the rise, largely in part due to the damaging emotional trauma.

Attacks like the one perpetrated by Sheldon Price are not isolated incidents and are occurring with increased regularity. 'Why' you ask? Because you stood by while the damage to these young minds was committed. You created these monsters! Sheldon Price was a test run. He was the first soldier we've deployed in our war. He is the first, but he will not be the last. You are unprepared and incapable of stopping what's coming next.

Monday, April 1st, will be a day where you will suffer unimaginable loss. This country was founded on the blood of Patriots and through similar sacrifice this country will be reformed. No school is safe. No state is exempt. No longer will we stand by. The system has failed them. This is our time to rise up and rebel."

The blonde looked defeated after delivering the message. She faced the camera and the normally verbose woman was speechless.

Wiz muted the television. "I think it's legit."

"Either it is or isn't. Why do you think it's real?" Jay asked.

"It's completely anonymized, and I can't locate the source. It's bouncing all over the place. This ability to hide their digital footprint makes me concerned."

"What the hell does the message mean?" Jay asked, scanning the members of his unit.

"Not sure. It sounds like a coordinated attack, but I'm not exactly sure how they plan to pull it off," Wiz answered. "I'm looking for other specific chatter on social media and the like, using similar phrasing. I'll hopefully have more for you in a bit."

"Well, it's going to be hard to filter it out after that. Everyone in the world is going to be talking about it," Jay said.

"Listening to the message, we can at least piece together a rough idea of what the plan is to accomplish," Nick said. "We know the date. We know the targets are schools, most likely high schools if the Price attack was actually a test run. And we know it's a large-scale nation-wide attack."

"How in hell could anyone pull off an operation of that magnitude?" Gator asked.

"He already told us," Spider said quietly, inserting himself into the debate.

"How so?" Gator asked.

"He said Sheldon Price was a test. Somehow, Price was mobilized to carry out his attack. Whatever method they used to connect with and manipulate him, they've obviously done with others," Spider said. "That is if this is a real threat and not some hoax."

"It could be a bluff. Or it could be someone using the shooting to further some anti-bullying agenda," Jay said.

Wiz was shaking his head. "I don't think so."

"Why not?" Jay asked.

"Because Spider's already figured it out," Wiz said.

"I did?" Spider asked.

Wiz nodded. "How do you connect with a teenager?"

"Facebook, Instagram, you name it. Take your pick of the social media roulette wheel," Nick said.

"Or this," Wiz said, pushing back in his chair and exposing the image on one of his monitors.

REBEL DOGS in dark red letters with an image of a wolf's head in the backdrop appeared on the screen.

"What's that?" everyone asked, almost in unison.

"It's a free online first-person shooter game," Wiz said.

"I'm not seeing the connection," Jay said.

Wiz smiled broadly. "You won't believe what the game's tagline is. Rise up and rebel." Wiz cued up the speech they'd just listened to and fast forwarded to the end, hitting play, *"This is our time to rise up and rebel."*

"Holy shit!" Nick said.

"Couldn't it be some angry kid? I mean, who would use a video game tagline in a manifesto?" Barbie asked.

"Right. I know it sounds fishy, but I seriously doubt a kid could've anonymized the message put out to the media. I intercepted it and tried to trace it back to its source. It's changing IP addresses every couple of seconds. That's some crazy encryption. So, on that alone I'm concerned," Wiz said, sounding impressed.

"Why tell us when? Why give us the Sheldon Price link?" Barbie asked.

"Good point. Maybe it's a bluff. Or maybe, whoever's behind this has no plans of following through," Nick said.

"I don't think we should wait and see. That deadline is a week away," Gator said.

"I need to make a call," Jay said, retreating to his office and closing the door. "And Wiz, send a message to Declan. We'll need to get him back here asap."

Nick's eyes followed Jay. He wondered who was on the other end of the line. He understood the need for secrecy but still wasn't comfortable taking orders from an unknown source. He caught Spider looking at him with his dark unreadable eyes.

"You can't turn it off, can you?" Spider asked in a hushed tone.

"How do you mean?" Nick asked.

"That need to know. It becomes as important as the air we breathe. The investigator inside you needs answers."

"The investigator inside me is dead," Nick said. "He was buried today."

34

Albert left school at lunch time. He went to the nurse and told her he wasn't feeling well. She'd called Susan Walker, his foster mom, but she wasn't able to come and pick him up. He knew that would be the case and had in fact planned for that. After being cleared to leave, he walked the short distance to his home.

Passing by the Shelton Public Library, Albert wanted nothing more than to slip inside the safe confines of its walls and become the Bully Slayer. He refrained, the orders he'd received had been very specific. It was Wednesday and a package would be arriving soon. Graham_CrackerHacker had told him the exact time it would be delivered. The timing guaranteed it would be delivered two hours before any member of his foster family would be home.

Albert sat anxiously in the window sill and waited, peeking out from the blinds. At 1:36 he watched as a brown delivery truck pulled to a stop along the curb in front of the cracked walkway leading to his front porch. The man walked to the door, carrying a large box. He rang the doorbell twice and tapped something on his mobile delivery device. The man placed the box down on the tattered welcome mat and turned and walked away.

Once the truck was out of sight, Albert scooted out to the

porch and retrieved the package. His heart raced with the excitement of Christmas morning, or more accurately what Albert had always envisioned Christmas morning to feel like. His recall of such holidays was dim and sad.

The package was heavier than he anticipated, and Albert's cheeks reddened with the unexpected exertion. He put the box down inside the threshold of the cluttered hallway. Albert's fingers tore at the bubble wrapping covering the exterior, exposing a benign cardboard box. He slit open the box and stared in awe at the contents.

Inside was a small metallic box. It too had been wrapped in a layer of bubble wrap, but this time Albert took extra care in tearing it. Off to the side of the device was a padded manila envelope. Albert pulled it out from its wedged position and ripped it open, freeing the contents. A black handgun and three loaded magazines fell to the frayed hallway runner covering the poorly conditioned wood flooring. A white slip of paper had fallen out and lay under one of the magazines.

Hey Albert,
Remember the instructions. I'm proud of you.
Your Friend,
Graham

Albert focused on one word in the message. *Friend.* A word he hadn't heard in such a long time that he'd forgotten its value. He folded the note and stuffed it in his back pocket. Graham had told him to burn the box and letter in a message he'd sent through his Rebel Dogs account, but Albert Hutchins couldn't bring himself to burn the letter.

He got up from the floor and went into the living room to retrieve his backpack. The weight of his books was comparable to that of the package's contents. He shouldered the backpack and put the gun and magazines back into the box with the bomb. Hoisting the box, Albert awkwardly ascended the stairs to his bedroom. He gladly set the heavy box back down on his unmade bed. He then dumped the books out, making room for his gifts.

Albert returned to the package, removed the device and placed it gently into his backpack. The cold metallic device made him nervous, but Graham had assured him the bomb would remain inert until he flicked the switch. He slipped the remote at the bottom of the box into the side pocket of his pack and then picked up the gun. The bomb fit snuggly into the backpack with enough room at the top to cover it with a book.

Albert walked over to the full-length mirror. He pointed the gun, taking up an action stance he'd seen in movies and video games. Albert had a diminutive stature but looking at his reflection in the mirror with the gun in hand made him look bigger. He felt an unfamiliar strength.

And then he thought of Andy Bloom.

35

Tobie Jones read the message from Graham_CrackerHacker. His dad had always warned him about chatting online with people he didn't know, but this message seemed safe. It was just a guy looking to team up.

Tobie accepted the link and joined the campaign. Graham's avatar was a ninja and it approached Tobie's character, DocDeath501. A chat bubble appeared, and Graham asked, "Are you ready to be a Patriot?"

Tobie read the question and was elated to have amassed enough points to move toward the game's final level. Only one kid he played with in his high school had reached that level—Darren Jackson. Tobie knew Darren and had always been nice to him, although never felt he really knew him well. Others in the school treated Darren poorly, and Tobie, never one to shy away from sticking up for the underdog, had intervened on his behalf several times. Most recently, his intervention had cost Tobie an after-school detention. A price he'd happily paid for punching the kid who had knocked Darren's books out of his hand.

"Let's do this!" Tobie answered through his avatar.

The screen shifted settings and Tobie's avatar was now stood facing a school.

"What's this?" Tobie asked.

"Patriot level!" Graham said.

"What do we do?" Tobie asked, watching the computerized students entering the building.

"KILL 'EM ALL!"

Tobie sat in his room and stared at the screen. It didn't seem like any advanced level stuff. It seemed strange. A timer popped up in the upper right corner of his monitor and immediately began counting down from three minutes.

Tobie manipulated his avatar and approached the entryway to the school. He didn't arm his character because none of the simulated characters had weapons. He entered the school, expecting some type of surprise attack. Nothing happened. The computerized students moved through the hallway in the same fashion as if they would on a normal day of school. He didn't understand the purpose.

"KILL 'EM ALL!" The message bubble appeared above Graham_CrackerHacker.

"???" Tobie typed into his avatar's message box.

"KILL 'EM ALL!"

Tobie only liked shooting games where bad guys shot back. This seemed uncharacteristically sadistic. Tobie refused to shoot. Even though it was only a game, killing unarmed noncombative characters didn't feel right.

FAILURE flashed on the screen as the timer ran out.

Tobie shook his head in annoyance and logged out of the game.

36

"Three days since we've been authorized to move on this thing and we aren't getting any closer to figuring it out," Jay said aloud, but most of his frustration was directed at Wiz.

Nick could tell Wiz felt the frustration. The group hadn't left The Vault since the authorization to seek and eliminate the threat had come down the invisible pipeline. Declan had returned and now all six members of the team were huddled over their respective computers searching for something that would guide their next move.

Everyone knew the best hope rested on Wiz's shoulders and it was evident in the fact that the hacker hadn't slept or showered in the last few days, barely moving from his workstation to relieve himself and add to his caffeine level. The stress of a potential widespread attack on school children had the group's nerves on edge.

"Something's got to break. An attack of this magnitude can't be done silently. There's got to be a link. But there's nothing of substance. The game is encrypted. I can't access it! Crazy stuff," Wiz hissed in frustration.

"Maybe we're going about this the wrong way. If you're right about the game being the link then what about the physical address?" Declan asked.

"What physical address?" Wiz asked.

"I mean you're trying to access the game's database, but what about a physical address for merchandising. Most businesses have one, right? We just need to locate it," Declan said.

Wiz looked up from his screen as if seeing the world around him for the first time.

37

The rain fell more steadily, soaking through Albert's T-shirt. It was a cold rain and he shivered as goose bumps prickled along his pale skin. His head was down, which was not unusual because he did his best to avoid eye contact at all costs. But his social oddity left him vulnerable. Ever since receiving the package two days ago he'd been more distracted than normal, his mind constantly wandering to the task that lay ahead. The only place he found any semblance of distraction was inside the sanctuary of the Shelton Public Library.

He rounded the corner of the building's familiar gray stone façade, having taken the shortcut from the school. Every day's commute from school to the library was filled with land mines of potential threats, all of which came at the direction of Andy Bloom and his horde of brainless minions who followed his every move.

The water dripped down his forehead and into his eyes. He entered through the library's main doors and the instant warmth from the entranceway's radiators fogged his glasses, blurring his vision. Albert stopped and removed them, rubbing them on the inside of his untucked shirt. He raised the cleaned glasses to his face, but before he could put them on a blur of movement caught him off guard.

Andy Bloom's fist struck the side of Albert's head. The unexpected impact knocked him off balance. Shooting pain radiated out from the point of impact with dizzying results and Albert staggered awkwardly away from his assailant. In his daze, he tripped and collapsed to the ground. Albert felt the crunch of his glasses, still gripped in his outstretched hand, as he attempted to break the fall.

"I'm so sorry I didn't see you there," Andy taunted.

The sound of Andy's clearly recognizable voice and scattered laughter from his cronies was too much for Albert to bear. He felt the tears welling up and fought hard against their release. He scrambled to his feet, retreating madly into the torrential downpour. Outside, the sky seemed to understand his plight, masking his tears with the heavy rain.

Albert ran. His feet clamored through puddles as he sobbed uncontrollably, hyperventilating from the combination of exertion and torment. He entered his home, slamming the door behind him. He crumpled into a heap, alone and angry.

Albert's mind raced. He only needed to wait a couple more days and he'd have his revenge. The Bully Slayer would show the world that Albert Hutchins was not one to be messed with.

Albert felt the broken glasses in his hands and attempted to put them on. They hung loosely. The left hinge was snapped, and the end piece flopped loosely against his face. He grabbed a piece of tape from the kitchen's junk drawer and did his best to tighten it.

Albert stood facing the mirror in the hallway. His image was distorted through the cracked right lens. His wet hair and clothes, bruised cheeks, and broken glasses gave him the deranged look of a madman. His chest rose and fell in dramatic fashion as he surveyed the image.

Why wait until Monday? He was the Bully Slayer! Albert thought angrily.

Albert ran up to his room. He dropped to his knees alongside his bed and wiggled his hand between the mattress and box spring. His fingers found the cold metal of the gun's slide and he pulled it free. One of the three magazines Graham had provided was already loaded into the gun, but Albert made sure he didn't chamber a round. He was scared it could go off while he was sleeping. The extent of his firearms knowledge stemmed from game play and carried little in the way of real-life experience. Graham had sent him instructions on how to load the gun through Rebel Dogs' message system. It seemed relatively simple. Once the magazine was clicked into place all he had to do was pull the slide back and release.

Easier said than done. Albert struggled with the slide and decided he needed two hands. He used his knees like a vice grip to firmly hold the base of the gun while he pulled with both hands. After several failed attempts and some cuts along the palm of his hand, he'd managed to retract and release the slide. Definitely not as cool as he'd thought, disappointed in his weapon-handling prowess. It would've been embarrassing if he'd tried to do this at the school on Monday. Satisfied a round was now chambered, Albert slipped the black Smith and Wesson MMP into the front of his waistband. The weight caused his pants to sag and he ratcheted his belt to keep things in place.

Albert looked at himself again in the mirror above his dresser. The grooved metal of the weapon dug uncomfortably into his bony hip and he adjusted it several times, trying to find the best position. He changed out of his wet T-shirt, throwing it on the ground and missing his over-flowing laundry basket. Taking a moment, he eyed the black butt of the gun protruding out of his pants before pulling on a dry shirt. Satisfied he'd effectively concealed Graham's gift, Albert Hutchins walked down the stairs and back out into the gray afternoon light.

The rain had stopped. It wouldn't have mattered either way to Albert. His mind was focused on one thing and one thing only, Andy Bloom.

38

"Oh my goodness! Look at what we got here!" Andy taunted as Albert approached.

This time as the gangly teen walked, Albert's head wasn't down. For the first time in a very long time, he held his head up high and walked with something he hadn't experienced in years—confidence. Sadly, he was bright enough to know the confidence exuded didn't stem from some inner growth but rather the gun tucked in his waistline, chaffing his right hip.

Bloom's followers circled around, smelling the potential for confrontation. They began jockeying for the best vantage point from which to view the abuse. Cellphones were in hand and pointed at the ready, preparing to film another embarrassing moment in the sad life of Albert Hutchins.

"I like your new glasses! Where'd you get 'em? Bums "R" Us?" Andy Bloom snarked.

Albert stopped five feet away from his nemesis, the one person who'd made his last three years a living hell. Five feet away stood the person he hated most in this world. His arms and legs tingled with the adrenalin coursing through his veins. Albert's ears pulsed with each beat of his racing heart. He said nothing.

"I asked you a question, turd!" Bloom began a theatrical swelling of his chest and flailing his arms out wide, welcoming the challenge. "And when I ask you a question, I expect a damn answer!"

"Break his face, Bloom!" a boy off to Albert's left yelled. He paid no attention. His only focus was on the person in front of him.

Time seemed to stand still as Albert made his move, shoving his hand into his waistband and finding the hard grip of the semi-automatic handgun. Bloom took a step in his direction, oblivious to what was coming.

The gun now free, pointed out toward Andy Bloom's face. It shook violently in Albert's hand as his nerves caused his body to convulse. He brought up his left hand in a meager attempt to steady himself.

"You think a pellet gun's gonna scare me?" Bloom looked at his group and smiled. "Now I'm gonna hurt you really bad!"

"No," Albert said, his voice squeaking under the strain.

"What did you say?"

"No!" Roared Albert. The shaking subsided slightly, and he remembered who he was.

"Albert, Albert, Albert, you truly have lost your mind," Bloom taunted.

"I'm not Albert," he hissed. "I'm the Bully Slayer, bitch!"

Albert saw something in Bloom's eyes. It was something he'd never seen before in his tormentor. Fear.

Albert never heard the gunshot.

Bloom fell backward and began rolling from side to side, clutching desperately at his chest. The dark red spread across his tan shirt. Agonal gasps filled the air, but no final words from his enemy. *This was definitely not like the gaming world,* Albert thought.

Albert looked around, wild-eyed. Most of Bloom's friends had scattered at the sound of the gunfire. Their loyalty to their leader was readily apparent.

Albert tucked the gun back in his waist. He stood over Bloom's writhing body until it came to a stop. He then turned and walked slowly back in the direction of his foster home.

39

"We may've gotten our first real break!" Wiz announced to the group. "Check out this video. Some kid in Iowa put it on Facebook Live and it went viral."

The group huddled around Wiz's workstation and watched as their resident techie hit play.

The video was obviously taken by a cellphone held vertically when recording. The camera man, who undoubtedly was a teenager, was not steady-handed. The amateur production quality didn't take away from the brutality of the scene playing out on the flat-screen monitor.

A tall, rail-thin teenager with a slight hunch was squared off with another more athletic boy. There were a group of students surrounding the two, taunting and laughing. The video appeared to be capturing the early stages of a fight, and from the looks of it, a very one-sided fight. It was clear to anyone watching, the gangly teen was the victim of this group's assault. The video footage was taken to further any damage inflicted through the speed of social media.

Nick and the others waited, assuming there was more to the video than a few teens taunting another. And then it happened.

Nick saw the tall boys body language change, taking a stronger stance and standing more erect. Nick watched as the prey became the predator. The boy had withdrawn a gun, holding it pointed out toward the clean-cut athletic kid.

The screams and taunts continued from the others circling the standoff, and included in that volley of insults was the cameraman's voice, recorded clearly. "Look at Albert! He brought a toy gun!"

All of the voices fell silent as the awkward boy with the gun shouted something and then the familiar sound of a single gunshot resonated through the speakers of Wiz's computer. The athletic boy fell back and the video became a disjointed whirl of images as the cameraman ran away from the shooter.

"And how does this disturbing video, although extremely tragic, help us?" Jay asked.

Wiz rewound the video clip to the moment the teen had pulled the gun. And paused it. "Listen carefully to what he says before pulling the trigger. I've removed all the other voices and isolated the shooters."

Wiz hit play.

"I'm not Albert. I'm the Bully Slayer, bitch!" The boy with the gun said. The words were clear.

"I'm still not seeing how this relates to our current situation," Jay said.

Wiz smiled, pleased with himself. "Everyone, meet Albert Hutchins. Or as I've better come to know him, Bully_Slayer#1."

"Bully Slayer number one?" Nick asked.

"It's his handle, or online gamer name. And would you like to guess what gaming platform he uses this on?" Wiz asked, cocking his eyebrow.

"Rebel Dogs," Nick mumbled.

"Correct!" Wiz exclaimed.

"Holy crap!" Jay said, excitedly.

"And there's more. Police found a bomb in his bedroom. A fully functional bomb with remote detonator. The FBI was called in. I've already scoured their evidence database and confirmed it was similar in design to the one used by Sheldon Price's attack," Wiz said.

"So, the threat is confirmed. And now we know how they plan to carry out the attack. But how do we stop fifty bombers scattered across fifty states?" Declan asked, inserting himself into the conversation. "It took us days to get to this point."

"I've got that covered," Wiz said. "Remember you mentioned about looking for a physical address for the Rebel Dogs' headquarters?"

Declan nodded and the others intently listened.

"I came up with zilch. And then Albert, the Bully Slayer, appeared on scene. He screwed up. He'd kept the original packaging the bomb had been shipped in. It was stuffed in his closet and recovered during a search. The FBI photographed the box, to include the shipping label," Wiz said.

Wiz toggled his mouse and clicked on a digital file folder, pulling up the label's image.

"We've got your address," Wiz said with confidence.

Zooming in on the label, the others could clearly see the return address.

RD Consulting
1187 US-83
Liberty Hill, Texas 78642

"You're a damn genius!" Jay boomed, slapping the computer wizard's back.

"Yes. Yes, I am," Wiz said.

Jay turned and surveyed his group like a quarterback calling an audible before the hike. "Spider and Barbie, I need you to take a trip out to Iowa and meet with our friend Albert Hutchins. You know the drill, and Wiz will get your credentials ready."

Spider and Barbie both nodded.

"Gator, Declan, and Nick are going to head to the address on that shipping label. Maybe we'll get lucky and stop the delivery of some of these devices." Jay said. "Looks like you get to take a trip back to your old stomping grounds Nick. Liberty Hill, Texas isn't too far away from Austin?"

"I never thought I'd be going back," Nick mumbled.

"Time's ticking. There are only two days left before the attacks are to take place," Jay said. "I'll make the arrangements. You'll be flying in a private jet out of Reagan National."

"Great," Gator said, shaking his head in frustration at the thought of air travel.

"I guess I'm staying here?" Wiz asked rhetorically, looking at Jay. "I know the answer already. Just once I'd like to get out there and kick some ass."

"You can take my ticket," Gator said sarcastically.

"Don't worry, I'll be here to keep you company," Jay said with a laugh.

Wiz rolled his eyes. "Now that I know Albert Hutchins' Rebel Dogs gamer handle, I should be able to access his account. If I can, maybe I can backdoor my way into the company's server."

Jay was about to speak, but Wiz spun and started typing furiously into his keyboard. He was immediately lost in a sea of coding algorithms.

The rest of the unit's members readied themselves for their respective trips.

Nick prepared himself for setting foot back on the soil where he'd recently been buried. He thought of the funeral and then of Anaya.

40

"Good afternoon, I'm Agent Russo and this is my partner, Agent Smith," Spider said to the receptionist of the Shelton Police Department. "I believe your department received word of our visit." He smiled, sliding his FBI credentials in through the slit underneath the thick, bullet-resistant glass to the officer working the desk.

The officer, a thin man with ruddy complexion, took the badges and wrote the information into his log book, notating the time. "Yes sir. If you'll have a seat. Hutchins is in with his attorney at the moment."

Spider and Barbie sat in the metallic benches of Shelton Police Department's main lobby. They'd done a little research on the small town of Shelton and its representative law enforcement agency. The town, with a population of less than three thousand, was protected by a twelve-man department. Not very much in the way of crime for the small town. That was until Albert Hutchins shot Andy Bloom. The officer at the desk looked tired, a sign the tiny department had been overwhelmed by the recent circumstance.

"Should we be worried that he's speaking with an attorney?" Barbie asked in a hushed tone.

"Nothing to worry about. In my prior life I've interviewed many a perp in the presence of a lawyer. We shouldn't have a problem getting the information we need," Spider answered confidently.

Just then, the secured door nearest the main desk opened and man in a light-colored suit exited. Spider eyed the man, assuming this must be the boy's attorney. The suit was stretched to capacity, filled by the man's large-muscled frame. He did not look like a man who was comfortable in such attire. But what caught Spider's attention wasn't his clothing, it was the scar stretching across the man's face and ending at his misshaped ear. The thick man passed without giving a glance in their direction.

As the lobby doors closed behind the scarred man, the thin officer at the main desk stood up and ran toward the back of the office space and into an adjoining hallway, disappearing from view.

Moments later the desk officer barreled out of the same door the suited man had just departed. He withdrew his firearm and ran toward the exit.

Spider and Barbie stood, bringing their Glocks to the low ready, unsure of what was happening.

"Son of bitch!" yelled the desk officer, exiting out to the sidewalk.

"What's going on?" Barbie asked as they followed behind.

"Hutchins is dead!"

"What?" Spider asked.

"His lawyer killed him. Choked him to death in the room and just walked out," the officer panted, frantically scanning the area for the killer.

A squeal of tires shattered the quiet of Shelton's evening. A black Dodge Charger slid sideways out from the police department's parking lot and onto Main Street. The desk officer raised his gun and then lowered it without firing a shot at the fleeing vehicle.

Spider and Barbie ran toward their gray Impala. Barbie took the wheel and the two sped off in the last direction of the Charger. Sirens sounded from the lot behind them, but they were convinced the understaffed and under-trained members of Shelton's police force wouldn't be able to keep up.

The good thing about Iowa in the early spring was the dust. There hadn't been a heavy rain yet and it left the roadways coated in the dried dirt of trucks and combines, vehicles that spent most of their days off road. The effect was a trail of dust kicked up by the Dodge's tires like a jet's contrail, enabling Barbie to find the vehicle as he navigated the flat landscape of his unfamiliar surroundings.

Barbie treated pursuit driving like mogul skiing. To avoid any and all obstacles one must look beyond, giving the brain time to make calculations and adjustments. The engine roared as she accelerated the Impala to speeds exceeding one hundred miles an hour. The traffic was light, enabling her to close the gap with minimal difficulty.

She nudged closer, closing the distance to a car's length away. Barbie prepared to make her move, but the Charger's engine gave it a boost in speed that her Chevrolet couldn't match and the black muscle car started to increase the separation again.

The stretch of roadway was long and straight with smaller roads intersecting from neighboring farm lands. A rusted Ford pickup was stopped at an intersection a mile ahead. The farmer pulled onto the road without yielding to the two high-speed vehicles fast approaching.

The truck's wide right caused the driver of the Charger to brake hard, kicking up a cloud of dust. Barbie seized the opportunity and closed the gap.

Barbie brought the Impala along the left side of the Charger. Her move was quick. She accelerated and whipped the steering wheel hard to the right. The front right corner of Barbie's Impala struck the left wheel well of the Dodge.

The effect was immediate. The Dodge had slowed to avoid the collision with the red truck. The perfectly timed Pursuit Intervention Technique, or PIT maneuver, spun the black Charger one-hundred-eighty degrees. The reversal of direction at the high rate of speed seized the fleeing vehicle's engine. Barbie completed the move by continuing her forward momentum, driving the front end of her Impala into the nose of her target.

Barbie accelerated hard, forcing the Charger off the road and down into a shallow water-runoff culvert. The vehicle and the large, scarred man inside, were now pinned.

The Impala's windshield exploded in a hail of gunfire. Barbie and Spider were already moving, bailing out of their respective doors and finding cover behind the rear of their vehicle.

A pause in the gunfire either meant the large man was reloading or on the move, or both. Spider pressed himself flat against the ground and took up a prone supported shooting platform beneath the right rear tire.

Barbie, in a tight squat behind the left taillight, raised her gun without exposing her head and torso. She fired blindly in the direction of the Charger and toward the last known position of the driver.

Barbie's suppressive fire gave Spider a momentary window as the large man exited the Charger. The big man's legs, now visible under the open driver's side door, made good targets for Spider's well-trained eye. He fired two controlled shots, each finding their mark and striking the big man's kneecaps.

The large man crumpled to the ground. Lying beneath the door in the crux of the culvert, he tried desperately to move out of the line of fire. But he was too slow.

Spider fired again. Two more shots. This time the rounds struck the man's broad shoulders, flattening him and rendering both arms useless. The large man roared in protest to his incapacitation.

"Drop the gun or the next one's going in your skull!" Spider yelled.

"Screw you!" spat the big man.

Spider never repeated a command. He'd found it lessened the desired impact of its statement. He waited, silently counting down from ten.

The big man must've had his own mental countdown going. One with a shorter fuse. He fired at Spider's position. The damage from the wound to his shoulder made his shots inaccurate, but close enough to be a threat.

Spider fired one round, ending any further negotiations or prospect of interrogation.

41

Tanner Morris sat in his office and listened to the newscaster's brief of the president's most recent address regarding the terror threat.

"The president has called for schools across the nation to close on Monday April 1st. He said this April Fools' Day will be one remembered in history, but not for violence. He's calling for reform, creating an oversight committee whose sole purpose is to come up with an approach to neutralize the rampant mistreatment of our student population with regard to bullying. He called his anti-bullying campaign the single most important piece in stopping the widespread rise of incidents of mass-casualty violent extremism."

Morris flipped the channel and another newscast showed images from anti-bullying rallies taking place across the country. A unified national vigil was planned to take place on Monday, calling for a moratorium on school violence.

Each channel carried some variant of that message. Tanner Morris clicked off the television and sat back, sinking into the soft leather of his James River Leather Executive chair. He closed his eyes absorbing the impact his vision had on the country's outlook. He felt contented.

His peaceful respite was interrupted as Graham entered unannounced.

"Albert Hutchins is dead," Graham said.

"Okay," Morris said solemnly to his son.

"Tank's dead too," Graham added.

"What? How?" Tanner Morris asked, sitting forward.

"A couple FBI agents killed him in a shootout."

"This isn't good," Morris said, rubbing the sides of his temples.

"I don't think it really matters much at this point. There's no way of stopping us now," Graham said confidently.

"Maybe it's time to shut this thing down." Tanner Morris looked down at the finely crafted desk, breaking eye contact with his son and avoiding his judgment contained therein.

"You've got to be kidding! Shut this down? Have you lost your damned mind? All the work we've done. The years of planning. We are so close," Graham said through gritted teeth. He began pacing madly in front of his father's desk.

"Look at all the news stations. Look at the coverage. We've made our point! Our message has been received. The world took notice and heeded our warning," Tanner said, still avoiding his son's glare.

"What about Wendy? Her death doesn't matter to you anymore?" Graham seethed.

Tanner Morris looked at his son. Anger flashed across his face. The veins in his neck bulged and his cheeks turned blood red. "Don't you dare ever question my devotion to her!"

Graham stopped pacing and squared his body to his father, seated before him. "You're not shutting this down. This is my masterpiece and it's going to happen with or without you."

"What did you say?" Tanner Morris rose up, shoving the chair into the wall behind him.

Graham didn't move, standing still in the presence of his enraged father's impressive frame. He pulled a gun from a holster concealed on his back hip. "Take a seat," he said calmly.

"A gun! You're pulling a gun on me you son of a bitch!" Tanner boomed. He saw the familiar look in his son's eyes. The same look he'd seen when he caught his son killing the neighbor's pet. He sat.

"Good. Now you're going to sit quietly and listen carefully to me," Graham said. The gun remained pointed at his father's chest.

"I know that look. You crazy bastard!" Tanner said.

"Not a very nice way to treat your only living heir," Graham snarked.

"As of this moment in time you're dead to me," Tanner said. His voice carried less conviction staring down the barrel of a gun.

"It's sad to hear you say that, but to be quite honest I think you would've come to that conclusion at some point anyway. And in the spirit of honesty—I have a little story to tell you."

"What the hell are you talking about now?" Tanner asked.

"It's about your precious Wendy."

Tanner cocked his head, confused at the reference.

"Your whole plan to exact revenge on her tragic death was misguided," Graham said with a smile.

"I don't understand."

"You will," Graham said. "You always loved her more than me. She was your little angel. All I wanted was a piece of what she had. And then you caught me in the early phase of my experimentation."

"Experimentation? You strangled cats!"

"Well let's agree to disagree," Graham chuckled. "Anyhow, I know whatever chance I had at earning your love died that day."

Tanner Morris sighed loudly, displaying his frustration with the banter.

Graham ignored his father and continued, "Poor Wendy was

picked on at school because she was fat. It hurt her. Wrecked her emotionally. Kids are mean. But not as mean as you thought."

"What are you getting at?"

"She was depressed, but she wasn't suicidal," Graham said.

"They pushed her over the edge. The kids who emotionally abused her on a daily basis ruined my little girl," Tanner murmured.

Graham shook his head slowly and deliberately. "They did hurt her feelings. And yes she was sad. But that final push didn't come from them."

Tanner's brow furrowed.

"I can see you're thoroughly confused. Let me help you connect the dots," Graham taunted. "Who convinced sweet little Wendy to take all those pills?"

"No!" Tanner Morris shouted.

"I can see you know the answer is true. I worked on her weak little mind just like you had me do to mom," Graham said, eyeing his father coldly. "It was easy."

"I'm going to kill you." Tanner spat the words.

"Shh. You're wasting what little time we have left on futile threats." Graham looked at the gun in his hand. "Remember when I came to you and told you I'd found her lifeless body? I do. I remember the anguish in your face. I treasure that memory almost as much as standing over Wendy as she took her final breath."

A tear rolled from Tanner Morris's eye and down his reddened cheek.

"So, now you can clearly see why I can't shut down this thing we created. It was never for Wendy. It's always been for me."

Tanner Morris launched at his son from behind the desk. His movement was surprisingly quick for a man of his size, but it wasn't quick enough.

One shot rang out from Graham's gun, striking his father's forehead, instantly killing him.

His body slumped across the desk. Blood quickly filled the beveled grooves of the etched wood of the expensive hardwood desktop. Graham placed the gun in his father's right hand, stepped back, and waited.

The office door swung open as Sarah Barnes ran in. Seeing Morris's body she stopped short, a look of horror on her pock-marked face.

"I couldn't stop him," Graham said. "He started yelling about Albert Hutchins screwing up the plan. He muttered something about failure and then he shot himself."

"My God! Oh my God! What the hell?" Barnes asked frantically. "We need to call an ambulance. We need to do something for Chrissake!"

Graham closed the door and locked it, turning to face Sarah Barnes.

"What the hell?" Barnes asked, obviously confused.

Graham closed the distance between the two, standing close enough to feel the warmth of her breath as she rapidly breathed in short fearful gasps. The accountant did not handle the stress of her current situation well. Her body began to tremble, and it excited him, not in a sexual way, but that of a hunter in the presence of his prey.

"Before you die, you're going to transfer all of the company's money into my account," Graham said.

"Do what?"

"You heard me. Open up the tablet in your hand and pull up the account. I'm going to watch you make the transfer," Graham calmly demanded.

"Are you crazy?" Barnes asked. Her voice quivered.

"You're the second person to call me crazy today," Graham

said, looking past Barnes as he nodded his chin in the direction of his dead father.

"If you're going to kill me anyway then why should I bother making the transfer?" Barnes asked.

Graham smiled. He smelled the remnants of Doritos on her breath. He liked those connections. He knew from this point forward that any time he smelled the nacho-cheese-flavored corn chips he would remember her death.

"You'll do what I ask because otherwise I won't be so quick about it. And you won't like that." Graham moved closer, his lips grazing the bottom of Barnes's ear. He whispered, "You won't like that at all."

Sarah Barnes stood frozen in fear. Graham had slipped a knife into his hand. It was his favorite tool and carried with it a sentimental value, used on his first human victim. He had intended to use it on his father. The gun was only meant as a control measure, but when faced with Tanner Morris's rage-filled attack he'd been left with no choice but to shoot.

"Please don't! Graham, I've known you for the last six years," Barnes pleaded, tears streaming down her face and her lower lip quivered uncontrollably.

Graham swiped his left index finger across her cheek. He stuck it in his mouth and savored the saltiness, feeding off her fear before taking a step back. He didn't speak, but only glanced at the tablet in her hand.

Sarah Barnes could barely hold the tablet steady enough to type in the banking passcode. Graham brought the knife up toward her neck as a reminder. Barnes made the transfer and turned the tablet to show him. Graham opened his account from his cellphone and verified the deposit. Satisfied, he slipped the phone back into his pocket.

He looked at Barnes and then at his watch, wishing he had time to play. Without a word, he swiftly slashed the blade of the knife across the woman's throat. Her eyes widened as her life ended in the cascade of an arterial spray.

Graham opened the door, eyeing the company's technical expert, Simon Belfort, who sat typing away at his computer station. He wore Bose noise-cancelling headphones. The volume he kept his speakers set at would be loud enough to drown out a plane crash. Graham exited his father's office, closing the door behind him.

Graham stood behind Belfort, who must've seen his image in the monitor because he startled and turned to look, taking off his headphones.

"Hey Simon, sorry to scare you. Did you finish the final message? I just talked to my old man and he's on board."

"I just finished. Here it is," Belfort said, pointing at the audio file's icon on his screen. "I've set it up so all you have to do is hit send. Just like before, it'll go out to all of the same news stations."

"Thank you."

"To be honest, I'm glad we're calling off this thing," Belfort said.

"Did you get my account linked to all the Patriots on our list so that I can send them the notification?" Graham asked casually.

Simon nodded. "Sure did. You've got total control through your login. It looks like you don't need me anymore." He chuckled.

Graham laughed too. "You don't know how right you are."

The knife slammed down into Simon Belfort's heart. Graham snaked his left arm around the thin neck of the dying man and squeezed. He enjoyed feeling Belfort writhe and twist. He enjoyed feeling the struggle subside as the game designer yielded his life to death's call.

Graham grabbed his laptop and gave one last look back at his tapestry of death before leaving the Rebel Dogs headquarters.

42

"Movement on the front door. It's the same guy I saw go in half an hour ago. He's got a laptop in his hand," Declan said. His message relayed to Nick and Gator using the same bone mic and earpiece system from the church takedown. Nick was on the opposite side of the building, covering the rear doors. Gator was a block down the road in a diner parking lot.

"Roger that, Ace. Do you want me to follow or stay put?" Gator asked.

"Stay with the building. It's the only known we've got at this point. We don't want to lose whatever's in there. After the guy clears the lot let's hit it," Declan said, removing his pistol and resting it on his thigh.

Both Gator and Nick acknowledged the transmission.

"He's leaving the lot in the same tan Mazda he arrived in. You should have eyes on in a couple seconds," Declan said.

"Got him. He just passed by my position," Gator said. "I'm heading your way."

Declan saw the big southerner enter the parking lot.

"Now," Declan said.

Declan accelerated his vehicle, meeting Gator's on a blind side of the building near the main entrance. Both men were out of their respective cars within seconds of pulling to a stop, their weapons at the ready.

Nick called out, "At the back door. Charge set. Ready for the count."

Declan took lead and Gator stacked up behind him, placing his big left hand on Declan's shoulder as the men staged by the door. Declan checked the door's handle. It was locked. He set the breaching charge. "Charge is set. Front is ready. Standby. On my count."

Declan paused, listening for any movement. Silence followed.

"Three. Two. One."

The blast cut through the door, splintering the heavy wood and separating the locking mechanism from the frame. Declan moved into the building. The interior was setup as an office space, relatively open in design and sparsely furnished with a few workstations set up. The layout was not so different from the Vault his unit operated from. He took the left side and Gator reading off him took the right.

They quickly cleared the main space. One man was sprawled in a pool of blood, laying on the floor by a computer terminal.

"One down," Declan called.

Nick entered the main room from a narrow hallway. "Rear clear," he said as he entered, facing Declan and Gator.

The three turned their attention to the closed door at the end of the work space. Declan took the left side. Nick and Gator stacked on the knob side. Declan slide his hand to the doorknob. He turned it slowly. It was unlocked.

Declan made eye contact with his counterparts and nodded. They acknowledged and mouthed a silent count. Three, two, one.

Declan opened the door and pushed hard with his left hand, swinging it inward as Nick and Gator immediately entered, filling the room with their weapons pressed forward.

"Clear," Nick said, surveying the bodies of the man and woman.

"All clear," Declan said.

"Mother of God! What in hell happened in here?" Gator asked awestruck.

"I don't know. But I'm kicking myself for not having you tail that guy in the Mazda," Declan said.

"Let's see what we can gather," Nick said as he looked back and forth between the three dead bodies. "One thing's for certain. Whoever did this is one sick bastard."

43

"Are they okay?" Nick asked, speaking into the phone on the table.

Nick, Declan, and Gator were at a Vault location forty miles east of where they'd found the bodies of the Rebel Dogs employees. The Vaults were staggered throughout the country, giving the unit the ability to operate at full capacity with fully functional op centers. Each Vault contained a variety of equipment and weapons to effectively carry out those missions.

"Yes. Neither of them was hit during the exchange of gunfire. Not so much can be said for the other guy," Jay said, from the other end of the call.

"So, I guess there'll be no interrogation for Spider to conduct?" Gator chimed in with a laugh.

"Not unless he can communicate with the dead," Jay said. "Spider and Barbie are going to remain in that area a bit longer. Hopefully, there are some clues that will help us narrow our leads. Albert Hutchins was our best lead. But now that he's dead we need to look elsewhere. The clock is ticking on this thing."

"Not sure where we go from here," Nick said.

"Well, I've been able to confirm one of your dead guys from

the warehouse. It was Tanner Morris," Wiz said in the background.

"Are we supposed to know the name?" Declan asked.

"If you read Forbes, then yeah. But from the sound of it, I would venture to say that's a big no," Wiz said.

The three men looked at each other and shrugged. "Never heard of him," Declan confirmed.

Wiz said, "Anyway, the guy was one of those young entrepreneurs who hit it big early. He crashed and burned after his youngest daughter died. Even did a stint in prison for a DUI manslaughter case. After that he'd supposedly made back some of his fortune but has been very reclusive. His only living family member is his son Graham. I'm guessing by the description you gave, that's who you saw leave the headquarters building, just before you entered."

"Maybe the son got wind of his dad's plan to attack school children and took it upon himself to end it?" Nick postulated.

"You might be right. Nothing is known yet. So, assumptions are all we've got right now. Wiz has been working to gain access to the Rebel Dogs server. Once he gets inside, we should be able to confirm some things," Jay said.

"You might want to turn on the news," Wiz said excitedly.

Gator took up the remote in his large hand and clicked the TV power button.

An animatedly expressive reporter was in mid-sentence, "—it looks like the threat may have been resolved. Our station just received another message and we're going to play it for you now."

The mechanical voice of the digitized audio file played:

"Our voice has been heard. The message has been received. Legislators have taken notice. Schools are vowing to take a stand against those students within their walls who choose to damage the innocent. The rebellion has turned peaceful for now. But know this, we are always

watching. Do not slip in your resolve or we will be there to remind you. Tomorrow, Monday April first, will come and go without violence. Your children will be safe to return to school. We're glad you saw the err of your ways and changed course. Your ability to do this has saved countless lives. This will hopefully be the last message you'll ever receive from us."

The news anchor, dressed in a dark suit and bright red tie, looked into the camera and smiled.

"Well folks, it appears that whoever was behind this threat had a change of heart. Schools will remain closed on Monday as law enforcement verifies this message and confirms the threat to our nation's children has officially ended," the anchor said enthusiastically.

Gator muted the sound on the television and the group turned their attention back to the conference call.

"Thoughts?" Jay asked.

"It'd be nice if this is the case. But I'd like to find Tanner's son and have a little conversation with him to know for sure," Nick responded.

"Agreed. Wiz is working on locating an address for him, but it appears he's more of a recluse than his father. The last picture we were able to locate of him was from a charity banquet, several years ago, before his father went to prison," Jay said.

"Maybe they never really intended to do any of this. I mean coordinating with students from around the country. Are there really that many angry kids willing to blow up a school?" Gator said, shaking his head in disbelief.

"That and the fact that this group announced the planned day of attack. Anyone in their right mind would assume school systems would take precautionary measures and shut down campuses. Who warns a target before a strike?" Declan asked.

"Maybe that was the point. Make some impact with Price and Hutchins and let hysteria take over," Gator said.

"Or maybe Monday was never the plan. What if all this was done to lull us into a false sense of security?" Nick asked.

"One thing's for certain, we better find Graham Morris before the school bell rings on Tuesday morning," Declan said.

The group fell silent, knowing their work wasn't done yet.

44

Graham Morris sat inside his motel room. It was a disgusting place located on the outskirts of Austin. He tolerated the substandard conditions—a necessary sacrifice, knowing the need to keep a low profile until he left the country after his masterpiece of carnage was completed. He'd paid for the room with cash and had already changed his appearance, darkening his hair and shaving off his goatee, to visually match his new passport and other credentials. A new life awaited him and with it, a new hunting ground for his animalistic desire. Closing his eyes, he smiled at the thought of it. Opening them, he put the thought of his future endeavors on hold. Everything hinged on tomorrow.

A few taps of his laptop's keyboard and he'd logged into his Rebel Dogs user account. Simon Belfort had given him unlimited access, linking his settings to administrative capabilities.

It was the eve of his masterpiece's unveiling, and almost two days had passed since he'd killed his father. With no further messages sent to the media and all investigative leads exhausted, the media was labeling the threat an elaborate hoax. This pleased Graham greatly.

Tomorrow morning he would prove them wrong. His father

taught him to never underestimate an enemy's ability until you've looked him in the eye. How many had looked into his green eyes in their final moments? Only he knew the number, a tally soon to grow exponentially. Everyone had mistakenly underestimated Graham Morris, to include his father.

The bright screen of his laptop cast its glow upon the dreary surroundings of his temporary living quarters. With twelve hours to go, Graham hit send on his final message, calling his Patriots to battle. His heart beat more rapidly in anticipation of tomorrow's culminating event.

Graham stared at the screen, impatiently waiting for the first response to populate Graham_CrackerHacker's inbox. He looked down at his watch. Several minutes had passed. This was not typical. The weak little pissants usually responded in seconds to any message he'd sent. Their pathetic lives were desperate for his friendship, like a desert flower waiting for the first drop of rain. And he definitely didn't expect this lag with the final phase already underway. He went into the message log's sent box, verifying it had left the digital outbox. All the messages were marked as sent.

Ten more minutes passed by without a response. Graham became unhinged, pacing the room wildly. Grabbing a cigarette from the pack on the dresser, he opened the door to step outside for a smoke. Halfway out, he heard the ding of his computer's inbox alert.

Graham spun and rushed over to the bed where he'd left his laptop. The message was from a familiar player. It was from a Patriot, but one he'd never expected to hear from again. That was because this Patriot was already dead.

Bully_Slayer#1, the user name of the recently deceased Albert Hutchins, had sent him a message. He hesitated to open it for fear that it might contain some malware capable of corrupting his hard drive. Curiosity got the better of him and he clicked the mail icon in the upper-right corner of his screen, opening it.

Bully Slayer's message, simply stated:

Graham, your attack has been called off. GAME OVER!

Graham stood up, throwing aside the computer. He ran over to the drawn blinds and peered out, half expecting to see a line of police cars and SWAT trucks. The parking lot was empty, minus a few scattered vehicles parked in front of the sparsely populated motel. These cars had been there when he'd arrived earlier. Convinced he was momentarily safe, he retreated into the room.

Frantic, Graham grabbed his gun and packed up his belongings. He picked up his laptop and started to stuff it into his suitcase. An idea crossed his depraved mind and he stopped suddenly, opening the computer and accessing his Patriot database. Seeing what he was looking for, he closed it and left the hotel room.

Graham sped off into the night, heading toward his only chance of success.

45

"How many do we have located and detained so far?" Jay asked.

"I already told you. I'm not getting these reports in real time. There are delays in the data entry and my ability to retrieve them," Wiz said, agitatedly. "Forty-four accounted for. Looks like we've nabbed all but six. No. Wait. I just got another message. Five. We're looking at five at large."

The unit's resident technical expert looked more haggard than before. He'd used Albert Hutchins' gamer Bully_Slayer#1 account to hack into the digital backdoor of the Rebel Dogs server he'd been data mining, searching for any links to Patriots. It was a terrifying realization when he'd found the threat had not been a bluff. There were fifty Patriots, from each state in the nation, with the exception of Iowa, where Hutchins had launched his attack three days ahead of time. Fifty children willing to attack and kill their innocent classmates. It was a scary revelation.

After accessing the server, Wiz had located the message blast sent to all the Patriots. The plan had never been to launch an attack on April 1st. The 2nd had always been the target date. Without Hutchins' screw up, he'd never had been able to tip the scale in their favor. They'd have been blindsided by the attack.

The Patriot list contained the real names of each player and their physical address. Each had been sent the same package Sheldon Price and Albert Hutchins had received. Wiz, through Jay's unnamed superior, was able to disseminate the list to state and local law enforcement. Raids were being run across the county and Wiz had been crossing names off the Patriot list once an apprehension was made. He was waiting confirmation of those last five still on the loose.

"I'm glad we left those guys in Texas for an extra bit of time. One of the last five returns to an Austin address," Wiz said. "Maybe luck's on our side on this one."

Jay looked unusually stressed. "I'd prefer the local agencies handle it. We don't want to expose ourselves unnecessarily."

"Still, it's always good to have a contingency plan should things break bad," Wiz said.

"Agreed," Jay said. "Still no trace of Graham Morris?"

"No. But he got the message I sent him. I got a digital receipt a few minutes ago," Wiz said.

"Well, he's priority one for every law enforcement agency in-country and his face is plastered across every news station. I can't imagine it being very long before he turns up in custody or dead. Either is fine by me."

Wiz slurped from his can of Mountain Dew and turned his attention back to his computer. "Jay, I think we've got a problem."

"What's up?"

"Darren Jackson is missing," Wiz said.

Jay looked over Wiz's shoulder, reading the intercepted transmission. "Where?"

"He's the Patriot from Austin," Wiz said.

"Send the information and address to Nick," Jay said.

A couple keystrokes later Wiz looked up, "Done. I also was able to locate a recent photo of the kid from the school's database. He's a Junior at Woodrow Wilson High."

"Let's hope he turns up," Jay said.

"And there's another problem."

"What now?" Jay's patience stretched thin.

"They did a search of Darren Jackson's house. Neither bomb nor gun were located," Wiz said.

"We've got an angry teen who's recently been radicalized and is now roaming the streets of Austin with a bomb," Jay said, letting out a sigh of frustration. "That's a recipe for disaster if I've ever heard one."

46

"I'm driving you and that's final!" Kemper said.

Tobie threw his hands up and stormed out to the car. "I should've never shown you that message! You're such a spaz! It doesn't mean anything."

Tobie had the day off from school yesterday because of the national threat. Kemper had taken the day off, hoping he could spend some quality time with his son. He'd hoped to reconnect with his son and break down the growing emotional distance. His plan had failed and Tobie spent most of the day in his room and Kemper spent several hours typing up his case notes.

The unspoken tension continued this morning, coming to a head when Tobie showed him a message from one of his classmates.

"Haven't you been paying attention to the news this past week? There's been threats to schools across the county. I'm going to alert your Principal and then check this kid out when I get back to headquarters," Kemper said, following after his son.

The two got into the Austin detective's beige unmarked Ford Taurus. Kemper sat and looked over at his son and tried to calm his voice, softening his tone. "Listen, when some kid sends you a text telling you not to come to school today. A message like that, coming the day after a planned attack, then, yeah, I'm going to be a little bit concerned."

Tobie gave his all-too-familiar roll of the eyes and said, "Dad, you're totally overreacting. Darren is a quiet kid. He'd never do anything like that. It was April Fool's Day yesterday! He was probably just trying to be funny and prank me. Something dumb like that."

"Let's hope so," Kemper said, pulling out of his apartment complex's parking lot.

Tobie tapped his finger on dashboard's digital clock and smirked. "And Dad, you might want to use your lights and sirens."

"Why?"

"Because we're going to be late," Tobie said, a broad grin stretched across his face. "Dad, you're going to be late to your own funeral."

Kemper Jones laughed out loud at his son's mock impression as he pulled the Taurus into the heavy congestion of Austin's morning commuters.

47

"Nothing. Declan used his Bureau credentials and made contact with Austin PD. The sergeant he spoke with told him Darren Jackson left the house around eight o'clock last night and hasn't returned. He was picked up by someone driving a tan Mazda. She told police her son had left carrying his backpack," Nick said, relaying the information into the phone. "The kid has since dropped off the face of the earth."

"Shit," Jay said. "We've got to assume the Mazda belonged to Graham Morris and that he is with this kid now. The only positive is, we may be able to kill two birds with one stone."

Nick looked over at Declan seated in the driver's seat. Sleep deprived, both men's eyes were bloodshot from the long night of searching. They were parked in the lot of Woodrow Wilson High School, where they'd been for the last two hours. Gator was in a separate vehicle near the lot's only entrance.

"Wiz just confirmed Darren Jackson is the only Patriot on that list who hasn't been picked up by law enforcement," Jay said.

"Then this is our best chance at stopping this thing. Once and for all." Nick said, hoping his words were true. To fail would be unforgivable.

"I know, but this move is a big gamble. Keeping the school open puts every one of those kids at risk," Jay said. The long night and frustration accompanying the lack of sleep was evident in the tone and crackle of his voice.

Nick rubbed his eyes and yawned. "True. But if we shut this school down now then Graham may go to ground. We'd be left holding our breath. Each day could be another attack, another school, and we'd be back where we started, in the dark and totally unprepared. I'd rather we end it here and now."

Another sigh from the unit's commander, "There's no room for error on this one."

"Understood."

"And Nick, good luck," Jay said.

"Luck has nothing to do with this," Nick said, ending the call.

The plan was simple. The best ones always were. The devil always presented himself in the details.

Gator was in position, parked in a spot under a tree located only a few spaces from the only entrance to the school's parking lot. He'd be responsible for calling out the arrival of Graham's Mazda when it entered. Nick and Declan were parked in the center of the lot. Two larger vehicles bookended their small sedan. They'd be the initial takedown team once the target vehicle came to a stop. Speed and the element of surprise would be the advantage they'd hoped to achieve.

Most of the student body had made their way into the school at the sound of the first bell. A few of them meandered by their cars, most likely caught up in their mindless teenage banter.

Five minutes later, another bell rang, and the few remaining students trickled into the red-bricked building.

48

"You can do this! You're the last Patriot," Graham said to the boy in the passenger seat. "I'm counting on you my friend."

He watched the teen carefully, evaluating his physiological response. His body trembled as he sat with eyes downcast, cradling the heavy backpack on his lap. Darren Jackson was weak, and Graham despised him. Nothing would give him more pleasure than squeezing Darren's frail neck until his life ended. But Graham also knew the only chance of redeeming any modicum of satisfaction rested in the boy's ability to complete this task. And so, he'd spent the better part of the night into the early morning hours motivating and manipulating the teen's fragile mind.

"I can do this," Darren said, meekly.

"Yes, you can!" Graham said, giving the boy a firm grip on his shoulder. "The world is never going to forget your name. You're a true hero."

Graham watched as Darren Jackson's posture straightened. He'd decided the boy was as ready as he'd ever be. He looked at his watch. The tardy bell should've already rung and most, if not all, of the students would be inside by now.

Graham Morris drove out from the side street, where they'd been parked for the last hour, and began the final three-block commute to Woodrow Wilson High.

49

The engine was off. Neither man broke the silence. Without question, Nick knew they were in the eerie calm that precedes a storm. The mental preparation before the execution of a tactical operation was important. Visualization had long since been an integral part of Nick's pre-mission routine.

The quiet was shattered with Gator's thick Louisiana accented transmission, "Mazda in sight. Two occupants. Approaching from the east."

"Copy," Nick acknowledged.

Both men readied themselves, adjusting slightly in their lowered seats. Nick inhaled deeply, oxygenating his brain and readying himself for combat.

"Targets confirmed. Morris is the driver and Jackson's riding shotgun," Gator said.

"Copy that."

Nick looked over at his friend in the passenger seat. Declan turned his head and smiled. The calm with which he faced danger always impressed Nick, and he was glad they were teamed up on this day.

"They're pulling into a spot two rows back and ten spots to the right of your location," Gator said. "Not sure you're going to have a visual from your position."

"Copy."

Nick and Declan waited for a ten count. "Moving," Nick announced as both men exited into a crouched position.

"No movement from the Mazda. Both targets are still inside," Gator called through his bone mic.

Nick crouched behind Declan and the two men stayed low, snaking their way to the row of vehicles containing the Mazda.

"We've got a problem," Gator said.

Nick and Declan halted their progression, taking a knee behind a Chevy Suburban.

"Heads up guys. An unmarked just pulled in the lot," Graham said.

"I thought Jay coordinated to ensure all agencies, state and local, remain out of the area. This was supposed to be jurisdiction-ally claimed by the Feds," Nick said.

"Well, I guess this guy didn't get the message."

"Where's the unmarked now? Disregard. I see it," Nick hissed. "Shit!"

"What?" Gator asked.

"It's Kemper Jones. And his son," Nick said, exhaling heavily.

"Well this will be an interesting reunion," Declan said.

"Obviously, Kemper wouldn't bring his son if he knew about the threat. His kid must go to school here," Nick said.

"What are the odds?" Declan asked. "I thought you had a penchant for bad luck, but this takes the cake."

"Apparently you and I aren't the only shit magnets in town," Nick joked.

The two gave a quick laugh. And, again, began moving toward the target, only eight cars away.

"The kid's on the move!" Gator called out.

Darren Jackson, laden with his heavy backpack, was ambling

away from the parked Mazda toward the front entrance of the school. He walked with the rigidity of a robot, moving deliberately as if each step forward required its own independent decision.

"I've got the kid. You two stay on Morris," Gator called out.

Nick and Declan maintained their low profile but quickened their approach on the Mazda. Gator's car screeched through the lot, rapidly closing the distance on the unsuspecting teenager. The noise of the approaching vehicle caused the boy to stop and turn.

Gator hopped out of the car, pointing his gun at Jackson. Immediately the big man from the Bayou began giving commands to the teenager. Darren Jackson stood frozen, his face drained of color.

"You don't want to do this, kid! I promise you that whatever he told you is an outright lie!" Gator's delivery was calm and controlled. His pistol pointed at Darren Jackson's head.

"I've got to. You don't understand!" Jackson screamed. Tears began to fall, and his knees buckled.

"Let me help you," Gator said, reassuringly. "I can only do that if you take off the backpack. Come on Darren. Please hear me on this."

The boy dropped to his knees. Sobbing uncontrollably, he unshouldered one strap of the large pack.

Nick and Declan, only two cars away, prepared to take Graham Morris. In unspoken unison, they both slowly raised up behind the Mazda, taking a point of aim at the back of Morris's head.

Declan boomed, "Graham step out of the vehicle, keeping your hands where I can see them. Do it now."

The plan had been to take Graham Morris alive, a request that had come down from Jay's superior. Apparently, in the world of politics, the decision had been made that bringing in the man responsible would look better in someone's PR campaign than showing the nation another dead terrorist. But the politicians weren't standing six feet behind a deranged murderer.

In the ever changing fluidity of a crisis situation, each action had a potentially dire consequence. Time was measured in milliseconds. And Morris's silent refusal to exit caused Nick to take the slack out of the trigger.

The explosion's blast wave knocked Nick backward, sending him onto the hard asphalt of the parking lot. The impact had a dizzying effect, and he shook his head to clear it. His ears were ringing, adding to his sudden disorientation. As he began to get his bearings, Nick scanned his surroundings. Declan was down, wedged in a heap near the Mazda's driver's side rear wheel. Either his friend was unconscious or dead. Impossible to tell from his position, but he hoped it wasn't the latter.

Nick's vision cleared and he saw fire and twisted metal in the parking space where Darren Jackson and Gator had, only moments before, been standing.

The driver's door to the Mazda popped open and Graham Morris casually stepped out. His face was bloodied from bits of shattered windshield, amplifying his appearance. Nick evaluated the man, deeming him the poster-child for lunatics and madmen.

Graham smiled, looking down at Declan's body, twisted and unmoving.

Nick suddenly realized his gun was no longer in his right hand. He must've lost it in the blast. Desperately, he scanned the lot's surface. A split second later he saw it, ten feet away from him under the front axle of a small red compact car. He looked back at Graham, standing over his friend with a gun in his hand.

Knowing he'd never be able to recover his weapon in time to save Declan, he did the only reasonable option that came to mind. A quote from Sun Tzu popped into his mind, *"Let your plans be dark and impenetrable as night, and when you move, fall like a thunderbolt."* The ancient Chinese master tactician and strategist had server him once again.

Nick Lawrence roared, launching himself at Morris.

The guttural scream and sudden burst of movement had the desired effect, causing the armed Morris to look up, briefly distracting him from his task at hand. The gun, no longer pointed down at Declan, was now pointed at Nick's large frame.

A shot rang out, the sound of which was muffled from the concussive auditory damage caused by bomb's recent detonation.

Blood spatter covered Nick's face, blinding him and causing him to crash head first into the Mazda's trunk. Nick fell to the ground.

Wiping the blood from his eyes he visually scanned his body for the wound. He found no gunshot entry point. He stood to face the gunman.

Graham Morris was no longer standing. He was now sprawled atop of Declan, blanketing him. Blood leaked onto the black asphalt, filling its cracked surface. Nick's brain worked fast to connect the dots, which immediately became clearer at the sight of the man who'd fired the shot.

The portly Austin detective stood with his duty weapon still pointed in the direction of Morris's lifeless body.

Nick stood still, looking at the detective, a man he'd come to trust and respect over the many cases the two had worked together over the years. More importantly Kemper Jones was the man who, one year ago, had saved Anaya's life. And here he was again, stepping up in Nick's time of need.

Kemper lowered his gun, holstering it as he looked in Nick's direction.

Nick watched as his brisket-loving friend visually evaluated him. Nick's long hair and blood-covered face added to his unintended subterfuge. Kemper's eyes widened with recognition. Nick smiled faintly, trying, without much success, to alleviate the awkwardness.

"Nick?" Kemper mumbled.

Nick was at a loss for words and only could manage a meager shrug.

"How?" Kemper asked. His voice a muffled whisper.

"Long story," Nick said. "And one you probably don't want to know."

A groan from the pile on the ground interrupted the uncomfortable reunion. Nick and Kemper each took a step back, Kemper's hand on the butt of his holstered gun.

Declan pushed the dead body of Graham Morris off his back and stood.

"How long were you guys going to leave this dead guy on top of me?" Declan asked, adding his trademark cocky smirk. "Oh hi, Kemper. Funny seeing you here."

"Declan," Kemper said, nodding.

"Is this your handy work?" Declan asked, looking down at the dead man.

Kemper nodded.

In the distance, sirens alerted the local cavalry's arrival. The parking lot of Woodrow Wilson High was soon to be a cavalcade of local, state, and federal law enforcement officers as they converged to jockey position for control of the scene.

"Probably best I get going," Nick said.

"Take our car. I'll stay with Kemper," Declan said, flashing his FBI badge affixed to his hip. "I'll handle the cleanup. There's going to be a lot of explaining to do."

Without another word, Nick retrieved his gun, holstered it, and hustled back toward the car he'd arrived in.

He sped by his two friends and out of the school's lot.

* * *

"Are you sure you're okay, son?" Kemper asked, hugging his son for the second time in less than a minute.

His son's eyes no longer held the contemptuous glance typical of his recent crossover into teenage angst. Kemper knew the blast had scared him, but it wasn't the blast he was worried about. Kemper Jones's son had watched him kill a man. Regardless of the evil he'd dispatched, witnessing the death of another human being was a devastating thing to behold. And one that would impact his son for the remainder of his life. A lasting impression worsened by the fact its execution had been carried out by his own father.

"Are you okay?" Tobie asked, gently separating from his father's embrace.

"Yeah. I'll be fine. But it's never easy," Kemper said, looking back in the direction of Morris's body, covered in a sheet of black plastic.

"Are you sure?" Tobie asked again, concern in his voice. "Because you look like you've seen a ghost."

Kemper gave a slight laugh and shook his head, "I think I just might have."

50

Nick and Declan regrouped back at the unit's Northern Virginia Vault site, the same location where Spider had conducted his interrogation.

Nick had a newfound respect for Jay, impressed by the way the former CIA spook, with technical assistance provided by Wiz, had been able to manage such a complex operation. The group, under Jay's adroit supervision, had thwarted the worst large-scale coordinated attack in U.S. history. Nick couldn't begin to comprehend the devastation the nation would've faced if Graham Morris had been able to deliver his payload.

One thing was for certain, this ghost unit, to which he now belonged, was the only reason there weren't images of thousands of dead children plastered across every news channel. The live feed from the news currently playing in the background only showed one scene and the headline read:

Three Dead in Failed Attempt.

FBI and Local Law Enforcement Thwart Attack.

The entire group had assembled around the conference table, minus one. The large frame and gregarious nature of the ginger-haired man from the Louisiana Bayou was absent. In the short time together, Nick had come to like and respect the man. Although, he realized that he knew very little about him.

Jay stepped out of his office with a bottle of champagne. Unceremoniously, he uncorked it with a loud pop. Each member seated around the table had an empty glass or coffee mug in front of them. Jay moved around the table, pouring an ample amount of the golden bubbly liquid. Jay filled his own glass and remained standing at the head of the conference table.

Raising his glass, Jay said, "To William Robichaux. He paid the ultimate sacrifice. His second death will be remembered only by those in this room. Today, we give him back his name and release him. Until Valhalla!"

The group slammed their glasses down hard. Nick and Declan followed suit. In staggered unison they loudly repeated the phrase, "Until Valhalla!" A reference to the Norse mythologic hall where chosen warriors, who die valiantly in combat, are carried to upon their death. It, or some variant thereof, was a common saying among soldiers.

The circle drained the contents of their respective glasses in one large gulp before placing them back on the table. Nick surveyed the remaining members, moving his eyes from one to the next. He'd silently hoped never to learn the full names of the others in this group. Especially if that knowledge only came ceremoniously through death.

"We need a name," Declan blurted, interrupting the silence with his comment.

The rest of the group looked back at the man. "Huh?" Nick asked.

"Seriously guys? You call these office spaces, scattered around the country, Vaults. The interrogation room is called The Cube. How have you not come up with a name for this ragtag group of dead men?" Declan asked, ending the somberness of the ceremony.

The levity broke the heaviness of the moment and Nick watched as tense shoulders and serious eyes gave way.

"We tried early on but nothing stuck," Wiz said. "Then we figured maybe having no name gave us an added layer of anonymity."

"Well, I for one, think it's needed," Declan said, adding his cocky smile. "If we're out doing superhero crap at least our team should have a cool name."

Jay gave a slight laugh, "Okay, what'd you have in mind?"

"I've got no idea. Hell, my old unit was named after a steak sauce. So, I'm probably not the best guy to ask," Declan said.

The group laughed. The weight of Gator's death lifted slightly.

"You already said it," Nick said softly.

"What do you mean?" Jay asked.

Nick looked out at the group. "Valhalla," he said, pausing briefly. "Think about it, we're already dead. Each of us warriors in our own right. Seems fitting."

A slow nod of approval worked its way around the table.

"I like it. So, if we're calling ourselves the Valhalla Group and I'm the one who called you here, then I guess that makes me Odin," Jay said, referring to the Norse God.

"Great! Someone else gets a cool nickname," Wiz huffed. "Since we're in a creative mood, do you think we could change mine?"

"No!" the group shouted, laughing at the hacker's obvious frustration.

"Valhalla Group it is," Jay said, banging his porcelain coffee mug down on the table like a judge's gavel. "Next on the agenda is to locate Gator's replacement."

51

The strange funeral service ended, and the group separated. Jay gave everyone a couple weeks to decompress. Declan was eager to get back to his loving wife and three beautiful daughters.

Nick had been given a new identity with credentials to match. Nick tried to think of somewhere to visit, but every fiber in his body called him back to the one place where he knew he shouldn't go. Texas was now more complicated than ever with Kemper's knowledge of his existence.

"How'd it go with Kemper?" Nick asked.

Declan shrugged. "We had a complicated scene to clear up and getting our story straight took a bit of work."

Nick gave a nod.

"Plus, I think he's smart enough not to ask questions he doesn't want the answer to," Declan said.

"Talk about poor timing," Nick said.

"Well, his poor timing is the reason you and I are alive," Declan said with a smile.

"True."

"You know the man better than me. Do you think he can be trusted to keep your secret?" Declan asked, his tone serious.

"I do. He's a good man and I trust him completely," Nick said.

Declan gave a thoughtful look. "Well, we are looking for a new member for the team."

"I don't think he'd bite. Not so sure this sort of thing is in his wheelhouse," Nick said.

"Okay then. Just a thought."

"I do have another idea on who might be a good fit, but I'm not sure she's ready," Nick said.

"She?" Declan asked.

Nick smiled. In that moment he realized where he'd be going for his respite. He'd missed the last opportunity to visit Pigeon, Michigan. This would be an opportunity to make good on that. Nick had been given a second chance at life, just like the girl he planned to visit. And he knew Wiz would be pissed off if she joined their group.

Because she already had a cool nickname.

MURDER 8

When a senator's daughter is found dead in a Boston alleyway, former FBI agent Nick Lawrence is called into action.

A powerful new drug has hit the streets of Massachusetts, and overdoses are skyrocketing to epidemic proportions.

Senator Buzz Litchfield's daughter is the latest opioid death, and he wants justice. Law enforcement is being told to take the gloves off; to come down hard on the rampant drug rings that have plagued the area.

Nick Lawrence and the Valhalla Group are tasked with taking down the distribution network, and must partner with Boston's elite Tactical Narcotics Team to get the job done.

But just as they're about to make a bust, things go south. And Nick realizes that in the war on drugs, corruption is everywhere. And nothing is what it seems...

Get your copy today at BrianChristopherShea.com

JOIN THE READER LIST

Never miss a new release! Sign up to receive exclusive updates from author Brian Shea.

Join today at
BrianChristopherShea.com

Sign up and receive a free copy of
Unkillable: A Nick Lawrence Short Story.

YOU MIGHT ALSO ENJOY...

The Nick Lawrence Series

Kill List

Pursuit of Justice

Burning Truth

Targeted Violence

Murder 8

The Boston Crime Thriller Series

Murder Board

Bleeding Blue

The Penitent One

Never miss a new release! Sign up to receive exclusive updates from author Brian Shea.

BrianChristopherShea.com/Newsletter

Sign up and receive a free copy of

Unkillable: A Nick Lawrence Short Story

ABOUT THE AUTHOR

Brian Shea has spent most of his adult life in service to his country and local community. He honorably served as an officer in the U.S. Navy. In his civilian life, he reached the rank of Detective and accrued over eleven years of law enforcement experience between Texas and Connecticut. Somewhere in the mix he spent five years as a fifth-grade school teacher. Brian's myriad of life experience is woven into the tapestry of each character's design. He resides in New England and is blessed with an amazing wife and three beautiful daughters.

 facebook.com/BrianChristopherShea

 twitter.com/BrianCShea

 instagram.com/BrianChristopherShea

Made in the USA
San Bernardino, CA
21 July 2020